This remarkable novel about a young man's search for the continuity of his portable life, among the ruins of a murdered past and in the face of a blank future, is rich with delights, insights, warranted sadness, and a longing to make sense of history.

TODD GITLIN, AUTHOR OF THE SIXTIES: YEARS OF HOPE, DAYS OF RAGE AND THE NOVEL UNDYING

Welcome to the nadir of post-employment, post-feminist, mediocre masculinity. Michael Levitin's wise, funny tale is brilliant in both its pathos and earnestness. You'll thank him afterward for this splash of world-historical cold water.

NATHAN SCHNEIDER, AUTHOR OF EVERYTHING FOR EVERYONE: THE RADICAL TRADITION THAT IS SHAPING THE NEXT ECONOMY

We've collectively torched the planet the last century and a half, men leading the ruination. Levitin's labyrinthian embrace of our follies, tyrants, cuckolds, and lovers, not to mention aunts who write postcards to Einstein from the gulag and stoned buddies on bikes in Poland, is laughter and memory layered over it all and delivered by a compelling, life-hammered voice you trust from page one.

JOE SHERMAN, AUTHOR OF FAST LANE ON A DIRT ROAD AND GASP! THE SWIFT AND TERRIBLE BEAUTY OF AIR

This picaresque novel allows us to explore not only Eastern Europe but gives us entrée into Berlin's expatriate scene and tenders a witty sociological analysis of the city's bourgeois-bohemians that is worth the price of admission. Michael Levitin, a journalist by trade and former Berlin resident, knows this turf well. This is an insightful, entertaining and multi-faceted work with something on offer for everyone.

KEVIN MCALEER, AUTHOR OF ERROL FLYNN: AN EPIC LIFE AND THE NOVELS SURFERBOY AND BERLIN TANGO

DISPOSABLE MAN

Michael Levitin

SPUYTEN DUYVIL
New York City

Library of Congress Cataloging-in-Publication Data

Names: Levitin, Michael, 1976- author.
Title: Disposable man / Michael Levitin.
Description: New York City : Spuyten Duyvil, [2018]
Identifiers: LCCN 2018033198 | ISBN 9781947980754
Classification: LCC PS3612.E9343 D57 2018 | DDC 813/.6--dc23
LC record available at https://lccn.loc.gov/2018033198

For Hannah

In memory of Sergei Levitin,
Isabella Yanovsky and Regina Possony

THE PAST IS NEVER DEAD. IT'S NOT EVEN PAST.

WILLIAM FAULKNER

PART I

ONE

THE POSTCARD

L et me begin by telling you about the time my great aunt Josephine wrote a postcard to Albert Einstein asking him to save her life.

It happened way up in the northeastern forests of Siberia, not far from the Arctic Circle, in a city called Yakutsk. Now to call the place a city in 1941 you'd be out of your mind for it was a settlement with one street corner and one traffic light and all the sidewalks were made of wood—loose boards, in fact, hewn by prisoners out of the nearby forests of larch and fir and thrown down haphazard in the mud where they criss-crossed and straddled one another, and when you stepped down wrong a plank flew up and hit you in the face.

No, it was no city that Yakutsk but rather some creature slumped out there like a half-frozen corpse decomposing on the edge of Earth. No railway reached it; the Russian road system hadn't found its way there either. The fort built by Cossacks three centuries before might have remained just that, a deserted bivouac, had it not hugged the banks of one great and fearsome waterway: the Lena River. Oh, mighty Lena! Some called her the longest river on Earth. Like an ocean she was that wide, with a deep, frigid, menacing-ly slow current that seemed to pull the whole world down with her toward eternity. No bridge spanned her darkness. She ran unchallenged, silencer of all tributaries, absorbing her defeated rivals on an epic journey that carried from the mountains of Lake Baikal to the tundra-frozen Laptev Sea and it was across her black shuddering surface, calm almost as a mirror, that the ship carrying Josephine Antonovna

1

Grunefeld approached Yakutsk one pale September evening and docked without notice.

The boat journey had begun on the emerald green Angara River, outside a collective farm called Barnaoul, and lasted about a week. Not that Josephine was counting the suns or the moons any longer. She had stopped keeping track of time—first the hours and days, then the weeks and months as well—when their train loaded with other unmentionables (Russians, Poles, Lithuanians and a withered useless array of ordinary Jews like herself) rattled out of Kovno, across Russia and the Urals, sweeping over the Asian steppe past a thousand impoverished villages each one as dirty and starving as the last, on its journey into gulag isolation. What Josephine remembered—what Aunt Josey would keep remembering and would never lose the memory of to her dying day—was the shock of being woken from her sleep on that warm June night when Papa's cry sliced the bedroom air: "Get up my dear, they have arrested me!" She opened her eyes and saw two soldiers with rifles hovering above her bed. The Russian told her to dress quickly; the Lithuanian followed her movements with hungry eyes and declared that she had a half hour to gather her things. Josephine reached instinctively for her lipstick and comb, then protested: "But there is so much." "Yes," the Russian replied in a tired voice as though filling out forms, "pack the butter, pack the marmalade, pack everything you have." With a swipe he tore the hangers from her closet and dumped an armful of clothes into an open suitcase. Josephine flinched at the sound of Bubi's shouts coming from the next room. "Pack a fur coat," the Russian added, "you'll need it where you're going."

The books, the photographs, Mama's jewelry locked up in the attic—Josephine left it all. All, that is, but the soap. She had been collecting soap for months, saving it in bits and pieces, of every shape and size. Soap's a valuable commodity during a war, Josephine thought, so she hoarded as much of it as she could until now as the pieces came spilling out of her dresser: the fat and the round, the long and brittle and even the dust-like crumbs of soap that descended like a waterfall from the drawers as she thrust her hands in, grabbing what fistfuls she could before smothering their oily fragrance in the suitcase with a blue blouse and two summer dresses. Papa stood quietly by the front door with three policemen as the soldiers walked Josephine and Bubi down the stairs. Their bags were thrown on the back of a truck idling outside Duonelaicio residence #9. Then Josephine clasped her invalid brother's hand, comforted suddenly by its long, lithe fingers with their ivory smoothness, and followed Papa's frame as he descended the porch steps into night.

* * *

Pressed into a tide of three hundred prisoners getting off the boat that evening, Josephine balanced her suitcase against her hip and struck a defiant pose as she left the dock. Her mustard-colored dress, shrunk from so many washings, now covered her body like a stretched out rag. She was small and wasp-waisted, not an ounce over ninety seven pounds, with a face remarkable for its beaked nose and two glowing, almond-shaped eyes—eyes, Josephine knew, that were best kept lowered as she and the other women were lined up, registered, then split off from the men and driven by lorry to their barracks in the woods outside the city.

The next day the women were placed in pairs, handed long iron saws and told to fell the trees. Josephine, who had not worked with her body during a single minute of her twenty four years, now spent eleven, twelve, thirteen-hour days sawing down trees so large that two men couldn't wrap their arms around them. In the first week she felt death near.

By the second week her hands were coarse, her arms and neck taut and her back was hardened stiff. Muscles sprouted like a suit around her. They covered every inch of her petite frame so that Josephine no longer recognized the woman she had become. She even began to suspect that she was no longer a woman at all.

In the middle of October the first freeze came. The temperature dropped to minus fifteen and one morning a guard called Josephine away from the group of women and replaced her saw with an axe. He led her along a footpath through dense woods for more than a mile until they reached the banks of the Lena. "Logs in the river are starting to freeze," he told her. "You must cut the ice off the logs, like this!" With a violent swing he tore the axe through the ice. The guard watched as Josephine climbed atop one of the icy logs, swung, slipped and fell. The same thing happened again, then again, and it continued to happen long after the guard left Josephine standing alone beside the dark trembling water. Over days, she gained her balance on the slippery logs, and countering her weight against her swing she began to hack away the ice. As the air turned colder Josephine hurled the axe with greater fury. She swung her arms wildly through the air, propelled by hatred, ripping with long savage thrusts through the layers of ice as if to shatter the skulls of the Russian men who had sent her here, who had taken Bubi and Papa away from her and torn from her—God in your goodness, she pleaded, let it not be so!—the dearest thing she had in this world. Josephine clenched her teeth until her gums bled. She cried into the lonely Siberian expanse. By November she was losing ground to madness and, she knew, to death. The temperature fell to thirty below zero as winds from the tundra lacerated her flesh, deadening her bones beneath her frayed coat. But what the cold stung most was her feet. The soles of her shoes had worn to a thinness of paper

4

and she could feel the freeze creeping up through her. One afternoon on the logs Josephine stopped and in a moment of clarity realized: without a pair of leather, fur-lined boots she would die before the winter was through. She had no money and no means to acquire the boots in Yakutsk, which left her one option. One opportunity only.

The next morning Josephine rose early before the dawn and hurried in darkness over the uneven road to Yakutsk. Ilya was in the butcher shop already sharpening his blades when she entered. They chatted; she laughed at several of his jokes, biding her time. Then Ilya, who was eager to get on with quartering the sow that had just been brought in to him, noticed Josephine shivering in her tattered boots and said, "It'll soon be forty below, Comrade. I hope you're ready for a winter in hell."

"That is why I have come to you dear Ilya," said Josephine. She asked him for a piece of carton paper, the kind used to box meat for delivery.

"And how will that help you, Comrade?"

"Oh Ilya, it will." Josephine held several chips of soap in her outstretched hand. "I'm sorry I have nothing more to offer in exchange."

Ilya waved his burly hand as if brushing away a fly. "Keep your soap, Josephine Antonovna," he said and pushed a tab of stiff gray carton paper across the counter. Josephine thanked him and rushed back to the barracks. It was starting to get light, the women were stirring in their bunks. An hour later the lorry came to take them to the woods and all day long as she struck her axe into the ice Josephine was plotting her words. Nothing more and nothing less than is absolutely necessary, she told herself. It mustn't sound like pity. Emotion, yes, but not pity. Let's just hope there is a chance, only a chance…

That night Josephine watched the women file out to the

mess hall. She was hungry; she too wanted bread and broth, but she sat in the frigid air beside her bunk and waited. Once the barrack emptied she dug through the worn lining of her suitcase and found the stub of pencil she had been saving there. She took the piece of rough carton out of her coat pocket and used a knife that she had stolen from the dining mess to cut away the edges until it was a rectangular, hand-sized shape. Josephine's fingers were pale with cold as she sat down then under the dim light of a candle beside her bunk and, pressing the stub of lead firmly, slowly into the carton, wrote:

Greetings, dear and venerable Herr Professor Doktor Einstein,
I write to you from depths of winter and despair at the Soviet Workers Camp in Yakutsk, Siberia. I was deported in summer from Kovno along with my father and brother, both of whom I have lost. Herr Professor Doktor, I must ask of you a favor on which my life depends, with the prayer that you will help. I learned last year that my former Berlin classmate, the physicist Valentin Bergmann, has gone to America to become your assistant. Please give this urgent message to Herr Bergmann: He must find my sister Elsa Krumkotkin, née Grunefeld, living with her husband Abram Krumkotkin in New York City—though I do not know where!—and he must tell my dear Elsa to send here a pair of leather, fur-lined boots immediately or her baby sister shall perish. I cannot hold out very much longer under present conditions. God's blessings and thank you Herr Doktor, for whom I shall be forever grateful.
Faithfully,
Josephine Antonovna Grunefeld

Exhausted, with the fingers of her right hand quivering, Josephine looked up. Her eyes settled on the flame that was barely flickering on the wall beside her bunk. Fragile, thin, ready to be extinguished with a gust of air, the flame seemed to hold all what hope remained. Josephine read back what she had written in tiny, compressed German print and realized that now came the most difficult part: She had no address. She knew that Einstein taught at a famous American university but she did not know which. There was nothing to be done. Josephine turned the card over and paused, confronting the blank gray space. Then she applied the pencil with intense pressure, pressure so great she feared the stub of lead might break, and on the middle of the card drafted three words in tall, capital, solitary letters. She held the card out distant from her face and recited its destination:

"ALBERT EINSTEIN, U.S.A."

The next morning Josephine awoke with a queasy stomach. She told the guard that she felt ill and needed a doctor, and she asked permission to go for that purpose into Yakutsk. On her way into town Josephine's pace quickened. She was hurrying, almost running, and by the time she reached the commissar's office she was out of breath. A young officer with a thin moustache sat idly behind his desk, squinting through a dishonest smile as she approached.

"Comrade Prikov, I have a letter to post," she said.

"A letter?" Prikov chirped. "And where would the letter be going to, my girl?"

"Actually it's—" Josephine fumbled in her coat pocket struggling to retrieve the card, "it's more of a postcard really, sir, yes it's… here it is!"

She handed the card to the officer who studied it with mild curiosity, turning it over several times unable to make out a single letter. It wasn't Captain Prikov's duty nor was he officially authorized to handle prisoner mail. Josephine knew this and as a result she came carefully prepared. She had bartered three days' ration of bread, the fabric from her summer dress and her remaining pieces of soap for the goods she now drew with deliberate slowness from inside her coat. The officer squinted, unable to conceal a grin as Josephine set the bottle of vodka and two packets of cigarettes on the desk. She looked into his steel-colored eyes and said, "Please Comrade Prikov, will you do this for me?"

Prikov straightened himself in his chair and puzzled once more at the German print. Then he leveled a violent gaze at Josephine, placed the vodka and tobacco in his desk drawer and, without a word, turned in his seat and tossed the postcard on top of a pile of sealed envelopes awaiting shipment to Moscow. With a sharp wave Captain Prikov motioned her to leave. Josephine gave a bow and skipped out of the office. She stopped at the doctor's where she complained of a stomach illness and received a note along with some pills to show where she had been. Then she spent the afternoon washing the prisoners' laundry, and the following day she returned with the lorry to the forest, to the well-worn path where she carried her axe to the icy logs beside the Lena.

TWO

I'M A CUCKOLD

Berlin, 2008

I'll come right out and say it: I'm a cuckold. I come from a long line of cuckolds. It's a disease in my family going back three generations at least and that's just the ones I can count.

No doctor has diagnosed us. It's not the kind of virus that shows up in any old blood test or cup of urine. The shrinks haven't cracked us open either. They tried cracking open Dad after his first wife ran off with the writer Dilinger. That was up at Dartmouth College, Dad was teaching classics at the time and when he collapsed the clinicians swarmed him; like a band of locusts they picked and harassed and bled him until they squeezed an article out of his case for a New England journal but that was it. No one named the disorder and no one prescribed a cure which is why I believe deep down in my gut (where I have ulcers growing although I'm barely over thirty) that the remedy to this illness, this syndrome or genetic trait toward cuckoldry or what you want to call it can only be found outside the realm of pure science.

Now I asked the Kaiser about it because before he started in writing his colossal script the Kaiser was a linguist and I figured a linguist could tell me some things, but all he could tell me were the facts. Cuckold is a French term, he said. It sprang into use sometime in the thirteenth century from the old French *cucuault*, or *cucu*, referring to the female bird whose dual habit of 1) changing mates and 2) leaving its eggs in another bird's nest earned it the scandalous repute of a "brood parasite." The Germans swapped sexes (as they're famously fond of doing) but kept with the fowl metaphor, the Kaiser said; their word "Hahnrei" stems from the old German "Hanreyge" for a castrated rooster. Other cultures however went more strident in depicting a man wearing horns: the horns of betrayal! When a man's woman betrays him the Dutch brand him a "horendrager," the Greeks condemn him with the barbed syllables "keratàs," while the Latins—those proud governors of masculine culture the Latins—share a word whose shame and implication are the same anywhere you go: "cornudo" in Spain, "cornuto" in Italy, "încornorat" in the forested mountains of Romania. (Even in my home state of California it's not uncommon to hear a Mexican stand up drunkenly from the table and shout at his amigo, "*Te puso los cachos guey!*")

Yet when it comes to the Jews naturally things get a bit more complicated. For reasons the linguistic community is either unable or unwilling to explain, yids lack not only a fair translation of the word cuckold—they lack the concept of the cuckold itself! When I asked the Kaiser to explain this to me he raised his dark paintbrush eyebrows and gave a shrug. I still don't know what the oversight says about hypocrisy in the sex lives of our ancestors from the East. All I know is that my great grandfather Mikhail caught the sickness in Riga a century ago and that it's been like the clap in my family gnawing at our collective groin ever since. Mikhail's son, my grandfather Abram, later got the dose in Prague; that was before the war and before Devlovsky "that son of a bitch" ever came on the scene. I was young when Devlovsky died but I remember his white pasty lips and the stink that filled the apartment on the day he cursed Dad with his final breath. "You lost your balls and you'll never get them back!" he spat, then midway through a cough, as Elsa stood crying quietly in the corner of their Queens apartment, he expired.

It wasn't long ago I went to see a doctor on account of my

own balls and the first thing I thought about was Devlovsky with those cruel green slits of eyes on the day he issued his parting censure. I was still months away from marrying Lotte so I knew it couldn't be the cuckolding starting but nevertheless I was feeling a painful ache down there, sometimes the ache was in the right ball and other times it was in the left so after three weeks of rocking on my seat, sweating and agonizing and unable to work as I stared out the window at the gleaming steel tower on Alexanderplatz, I went to see a specialist.

I found the urologist Doktor med. Philip Kropf's office out in far western Berlin at the negligible tip of Kurfürstendamm. Now I've got nothing against the doctors in the East. The East is after all where I was living, it was my home, and I could have just as easily rung up the urologist who worked out of his Prenzlauer Berg penthouse on Heinrich-Roller-Strasse around the corner from my flat. But I knew that urologist and I knew he'd been trained under the hammer and compass of the GDR whereas in matters concerning ulcers and testicles and so on I feel safer in hands schooled under the Marshall Plan. And in any case I had a good feeling about Herr Dr. med. Kropf because he was unusually jovial for a German medic. He had healthy reddish cheeks and two bright glowing blue discs for eyes that shined with proud command as he gobbed his finger full of jelly and stuck it up my arse. Then he diddled it around a while asking, "*Und hier? Und hier?*"

"Sharp pain," I said. The Herr Dr. nodded and disengaged his finger. His gloves came off in a triumphant snap and with a face brimming confidence he said,

"Herr Krumm, have you visited recently a sauna or a veerpool?"

"A what?"

"A sauna or a *veer*pool, a spa, you know, vith a *veer*pool."

I thought for a moment and nodded. The previous winter Lotte and I had gone to swim a half dozen times at an old piss-blue Soviet-era pool complex that was tucked down among the gray corridors of *Plattenbau* near Jannowitz Bridge. I remembered sitting in a jacuzzi with a whirlpool but what I remembered more was sweating naked on a sauna bench as the Germans clustering around me massaged their pale folds of flesh.

"But Doktor my problem—"

"Yes, yes, you have contracted a rare bacterium in your prostate that is found almost exclusively in the public saunas and veerpools," he said.

"You see there's this gene I'm worried about—"

"The bacterium svims up inside you, settles in your prostate and *that* is vat causes the sore feeling in your testicles. It is only prostatis, Herr Krumm, nothing more."

I watched Herr Dr. Kropf scribble out a prescription for eight weeks of palm oil extract. Then, almost as an afterthought, his eyes shot up from the desk and aimed straight into mine. "Remember!" he said. "To cure properly it is very important that you ejaculate *tvice a day* for eight weeks. You must stimulate and strengthen the prostate vith the regular fresh flow of semen!"

I felt a rush of joy bordering on exhilaration. It's no cuckold's disease, I laughed, just bacteria swimming around inside my balls, thank God! Feeling blissfully acquitted, I dashed down the Ku'damm and boarded a Ring train to get back and share the news with Lotte. But Lotte wasn't home. Her theater company was in mad days of rehearsal for a show that was opening in two weeks. She wouldn't be back before midnight and by then, I knew, she would be exhausted. So, in my eagerness to start in on the Doktor's prescription, I committed the act that presaged my fall.

Easy Wayne had been pushing the site on me for months.

He couldn't shut up about it; he was like a pimp that way, relentless, campaigning to get me hooked the way he and Alan and the boys were hooked. Up to then I had resisted because up until that moment I still believed Lotte and I had a future. Never mind that our passion had receded like a noon tide; it all still remained somehow hopeful, a quiet and predictable slog toward the finish line—we were almost married for chrissakes! But then, with paper towel in hand, I scooted my recliner seat forward, pressed the on switch, jogged the mouse and clicked effortlessly, thoughtlessly, unheeding of consequences as I arrived at the site with its "I Agree" registry for users over eighteen. I paused a moment, waiting to hear Lotte's feet pattering up the stairs. But the stairwell was silent. The lights in the apartment were dim, all but the screen radiating there in front of me, and with Herr Doktor med. Philip Kropf's prescribed cure thronging in my consciousness, I began my descent into internet porn addiction.

That was the day I stopped fucking Lotte regularly, and soon stopped fucking her altogether. It wasn't the sort of cure I expected but it was the one I got, and perhaps most remarkable was the way that Lotte barely seemed to notice any change had occurred at all. It was as if she'd planned her own sexual retreat to coincide with mine, deft and considered; in a way, flawless. Thus I triggered the onset of an illness that has plagued my family ever since the unfortunate incident which caused my great grandfather Mikhail to flee Riga just days before the failed 1905 uprising.

THREE

MISHA WEARS THE HORNS

Riga, 1905

M ikhail Jakobovich considered himself an honest man.
Some called him a thoughtful man. What he inargu-
ably was was a business man. He turned up one gray morning in Riga just shy of twenty three from a village buried
in the bowels of the Russian empire. Having completed his
apprenticeship with a trader there, Mikhail considered it was
time to make his mark so he picked the world's busiest timber port and Russia's third mightiest center of industry to do
it. Riga's growth at the time depended on two big commod-
ities: flax, a long silky bast fiber used for making linen, and
hemp, a tougher fiber used for making rope. Manufacturers
were devouring flax and the shipping interests couldn't buy
enough rope. Mikhail saw his chance and acted fast. First
he contacted the men who held the purses. Then he gained
the trust of those who controlled the permits and the docks.
He studied the transports, learned which men were the important ones to know and which were not, and paid close
attention especially to those whose business interests lay in
London and New York and Abroad. The word Abroad, for
Mikhail, contained in it the sweet coherent syllables of the
future, for somewhere beneath his rough country skin there
was a voice telling Mikhail that if he wanted to amount to
anything in this life, he must leave Russia. But in order to
get Abroad, he knew he must first succeed in establishing for
himself a small name, if not the tidy beginnings of a fortune
as well. So Mikhail Jakobovich did what clever migrant yids

like him have been always doing: He learned how the engine of trade worked and then he went about improving it.

By twenty five, Mikhail, or Misha as he told his associates to call him, was settled comfortably in the Latvian capital. He traveled every week by coach into remote parts of the countryside where he spent long afternoons chatting with the peasants and negotiating his purchases of hemp and flax. Misha felt a natural bond with the landsmen for the simple reason that he came from them—from the rural districts and villages where he had learned to listen to their stories, to inquire about their health, to talk about the crops and seasons. He never tried to cheat the peasants; rather, he offered them consistent rates and was repaid with a growing turnover of orders and guarantees for delivery. Misha watched with pride as the giant merchant ships set sail for London and the capitals stocked with a portion of his goods. And when he wasn't arranging deals at port he was soaking up the charm of his adopted city, "little Paris" they called it, where the sounds of Latvian, Yiddish, Russian, Swedish and German mingled on the cobblestone streets beneath the Renaissance facades, Baroque cupolas and Jugendstil columnar grandeur that defined this new Baltic imperium. Yes! Riga was aglow, and Misha was glowing in it. Then, in the summer of 1903, he married.

Anna Djukevalnis was a ferociously attractive woman. A Latvian Jewess with long dark hair and restless, wide-set eyes, she came from an established banking family to which Misha had closely allied himself. Thus it was in their first year of marriage that Misha considered not only his success and his reputation but even his happiness to be within reach. Yet for reasons he could not explain to himself or to her, an uncalm was shifting in his bones. During their evening strolls along the coppery Daugava River, Misha would inhale deep breaths of the damp salt air and look wistfully in the direction of the sea as he pressed Anna with his singular goal: London. "Let us leave this place, my love," he told her. "Business will be bigger, life will be better *for people like us* in London." Misha spoke excitedly and constantly about the Victorian hub with its endless possibilities and the new life he envisioned building for them there. The move to London was becoming an obsession. But whether he chose to ignore or simply failed to observe his wife's cold composure, the truth is that Anna had no desire to leave her place of birth. The couple began to see the world through different eyes and, more quickly than either of them anticipated, they started to drift apart. Their walks together along the Daugava grew scarce. Misha spent longer periods away on business.

And then it happened.

Due to a disruption in the trains caused by an artillery plant strike, Misha returned home a day earlier than expected and when he unlocked the door and stepped into the living room he confronted a shocking scene: There, with his pants around his ankles, stood a bear-sized man, frighteningly larger than Misha, with sweat streaming down his forehead and his eyes pressed tightly shut as he rode with urgent, mechanical thrusts into the backside of Misha's wife. Anna lay doubled over the couch and amid the grunts and thrusts of her partner it was several moments before she lifted her face and shot her husband two horror-stricken, accusatory eyes. The eyes screamed with rage, not shame, and this, for Mikhail Jakobovich, was the unforgivable distinction. He did not hesitate long enough to think but grabbed a poker from the fireplace and with one deft swing he sank the iron hook into the back of the big man's skull. The man collapsed behind the couch as blood rushed from the hole in his head and spread in a thick dark film across the floorboards. Misha looked at what he had done, cast a sorrowful glance at his wife and walked out of the house. Then he stepped into a cab parked nearby on the street, handed the driver 150 lats and ordered to be driven at top speed to the station where, unseen by anyone of importance, he boarded the first train south.

* * *

Now with the pogroms crackling the way they were, 1905 was no time for a flax-dealing yid to be out wandering the Russian empire so Misha, after a quick scan of his options, returned to his native province. To his good fortune, the uprising that had recently begun in St. Petersburg demanded the full attention of the Czar's police units, thus all searches for the Riga murderer were quickly abandoned. Misha grew out his beard. He borrowed money from a trader he once knew. Then he faded back into the patchwork of swampy fields and villages that were so familiar to him and restarted business as though nothing whatsoever remarkable had occurred.

Inside, however, Mikhail sensed he was a ruined man. Not only psychologically but, more astonishing it seemed, on a physical, almost biological level he noticed a transformation taking place. The memory of his impassioned act haunted him. It hung about him like a heavy silhouette, pressing down each day with greater weight and causing him to hunch. Misha's breaths drew shorter, his eyesight dimmed and one morning he thought he felt two small, calloused lumps beginning to emerge like the blunted knobs of goat horns on his head. Yes, he was sure of it, there were stubs now growing out of him, they were pushing up his hat at odd angles and in conversations with clients, even with his friends, the horns were becoming an impossibility to ignore. Would God have visited Mikhail Jakobovich in those first mournful months following his crime and revealed to him its price—that every son born from his seed, and every son of all his sons thereafter, must suffer his fate; that is to say, that all Krumkotkins would be inheritors to the cuckold's curse—then surely I wouldn't be here today to tell the story.

But God did not visit him. God made all the signs that He was ignoring Misha, whose life carried on at a joyless and barely noticeable pace until one evening, after a tiring journey through the western villages in his province, he stopped outside an inn where a woman's baritone laugh caught his ear. Misha had been now three years atoning for his sin. He had put on weight. His eyes were gray, sullen, unhopeful. Yet that evening he decided with a gallant thirst for life to order rounds of mead and plum brandy for every peasant and trader at the inn. Song and laughter spread through the place and Misha drank heavily with the locals who treated him as one of their own. Then, in the wee hours when he felt around inside his pocket and realized he hadn't a key, Misha leaned toward the barmaid, the one with the wholesome laugh, and said, "Now, miss, I believe it is time for you to show me to my room."

"You're right to call me miss," the woman said smiling, "but better if you call me Dusya."

The woman led Misha up a narrow staircase and into a cramped room where she proceeded to help him off with his shoes. Dusya was strong and squarely built. She had a full chest, broad shoulders and hands with meaty nubs of fingers attached to them. In the pre-dawn light, through his alcoholic stupor, Misha beheld a woman whose brow was as frank and firm as the earth he walked on, and his nature overtook him. He pulled Dusya down with him into the bed and buried himself in her bosomy warmth. She offered herself generously, without doubt or resistance, as Misha swallowed her in an outburst of lust that competed with the crowing of the morning cocks. Shouts continued in the tavern below with

18

singing, broken glass and chairs overturned. But upstairs in their dawn embrace, Misha and Dusya dreamt together in delicious and uninterrupted sleep.

When the morning light pierced his eyes, Misha awoke and found himself alone. After fumbling around the room to collect his things, he hurried downstairs. The tavern's floor had been swept, the chairs and tables rearranged. Not knowing what else to do Misha left his payment on the bar along with a note: *I will return!* The following week he reappeared in the village, and on his third visit he spoke with the old bearded innkeeper, Schulmann, who was Dusya's father. Then, before the moon's cycle had passed, Misha proposed, married and hauled Dusya up the Dnieper River to the regional capital of Smolensk where he set about rebuilding his psyche.

Four

A Jew In Berlin

I wasn't always a disposable man. I'm not even sure how or when I became one. It isn't as if the condition hit me overnight—I didn't just wake up one morning to the baffling phenomenon like some Gregor Samsa—no, becoming disposable was something that happened gradually, it was a slow evolutionary ride down, bred into me and reinforced in such small doses that I almost didn't notice it occurring until the day I realized, quite simply, that I had become obsolete. I could feel my extinction coming on and was protestless to stop it. The absence of duty or requirements or a purpose of any kind may be what finally convinced me: the fact that I had no place to be and no time I had to be there. I wasn't in any great discomfort about it. It wasn't discomfort exactly. All I know is I had become disposable because I had lost, or more accurately had failed to discover, my function. I was functionless, that is, useless. But allow me with the Kaiser's help to clarify.

The Kaiser explains it all better, see, because he's the one who got all this talk about our generation of disposable men banging around my head to begin with. The Kaiser called himself disposable and he called me disposable too because he said men in our time have lost the appetite for being men. He said we've grown weak, soft, with little to say and nothing to do, like a bunch of commas folded in on ourselves, missing life's exclamation because we have lost the desires and abilities and qualities of men. Oh, the Kaiser has it all figured out, he talks about annihilated hopes and exhausted ambitions and no ladders worth climbing and all that sort of thing. He has even come up with a definition in the colossal text he's writing on the subject where he defines disposable as: 1) free to be used as the occasion requires (ie. not assigned to any special use) and 2) capable of being disposed of easily (ie. designed to be thrown away). Both definitions imply potential use—use in the future or use in the past—but what they really mean, what disposable means for men like me and men like the Kaiser who are aching with the male potential inside us, is uselessness.

Here though I'm getting ahead of myself because it wasn't until November of that matrimonial year 2008, after the bottom fell out from the global economy, after America elected its first black president and after I observed Herr Doktor med. Philip Kropf's prescription to flush the bacterium from my balls through twice daily ejaculation, that Lotte kicked me out and I fell ill. I was living at the time in a crumbling Soviet flat on the lower end of the Allee. Not Kastanienallee or Schönhauser Allee but their ugly cousin, Prenzlauer Allee. The Allee was a noisy boulevard punched with shwarma stands and shadowy *Kneipe* bars where men went to drink all day, and it ripped a gash through the genteel calm of Prenzlauer Berg. Most flats on the Allee were like mine: spacious rotting leftovers from the German Democratic Republic that no one had bothered to clean, renovate, redesign or even think about for the last forty five years. The rent was low but there were hidden costs. Half the electrical sockets didn't work. Cold air came whistling through the wobbly window frames. The shower was a thin nozzle balanced between two rusted pipes holding up the water tank. To top it off, the flat's only heat came from a cracked ceramic coal oven anchored in the corner of the bedroom. I would have hunted longer for a place but Lotte didn't give me a choice. She just announced, clean and decisive one morning over breakfast:

Wolfgang's moving in.

I remember sitting there, limply holding the butter knife as I prepared to spread some *Quarkkäse* on my Brötchen, thinking Wolfgang from Düsseldorf? You're leaving me for a whiny femme director with big frame glasses and a hideous laugh? I remembered meeting him once after a play he directed at the Gorki. It was pumped full with dreary monologues and the usual German bouts of screaming and nudity. When Lotte introduced me to Wolfgang after the show I noted the way his narrow glittery eyes completely avoided mine. Lotte was hungry for ascent. She craved the ladder with its endless rungs so I thought nothing of all the titters and compliments she laid on Wolfgang that night; he was just another droll theater man Lotte was sizing up to capture like every unhinged actress in Berlin.

But with those three words, *Wolfgang's moving in*, there was nothing more to say. Lotte had snared her prey and I won't lie saying that her announcement caught me wholly by surprise. An intuitive fear—my foresight, perhaps, as a man genetically predisposed to cuckoldry—had braced me for the shock. It was bound to happen, I figured, if not with the lavishly turtlenecked Wolfgang then with some other strutting auteur. So I finished applying my *Quarkkäse* and calmly ate the bread roll while I digested Lotte's remark, and three days later I abandoned our lofty apartment overlooking Zionskirchplatz and dragged my bags several cobblestoned blocks to the Allee. I'd responded to an online post from a man named Eduardo who was subletting his place. After I arrived, we shivered together for some time in his kitchen next to the open-lit gas stove, smoking cigarettes and sipping from tiny cups of Turkish coffee. Eduardo told me he was returning to Santiago to live with his mother and revise an unpublished novel he had been working on for nine years. We discovered we shared a mutual admiration for Bolaño and Almodovar. Eduardo wrote down a number on a piece of paper that I was to call to order coal. Then he abruptly stood up, handed me the keys and with a solemn wave stepped out the door, leaving me alone in the gray November light.

Less than twelve hours later the contagion gripped me like no sickness I had experienced before. It started a bit like the way that they described it in the New England journal article about Dad, whose first symptom was a debilitating rush of cold. Eduardo's flat, as I explained, had the infrastructure of a GDR prison cell, so I fetched the scrap of paper and used my remaining strength to dial the coal company. I was nearly unconscious when the delivery man showed up the next day with his flatbed truck and humped half a ton of the filthy black lumps down into the cellar in a wicker basket that he carried on his back. The man was short and taut with wizened features like one of Bruegel's men. His back caved with the weight of years and his face was frozen in a painful grimace, but when he entered my apartment to collect the ninety euro fee, his gentle smile told me I was the sicker man.

That evening I collapsed. The cold had metamorphosed into heat and suddenly I was engulfed in fever. My skin turned red, my limbs ached, I couldn't stop sweating, on top of that my eyes were on fire, bulging off my face to the point I couldn't see. For days I flopped around on a mattress beside the coal oven, writhing under a mountain of Eduardo's blankets. The days turned into weeks and before I knew it I had missed the noxious fanfare of Berlin's Christmas markets. I even missed Christmas itself. All day long I heard the race of car traffic beneath my window, the impatient beeping sound of *Strassenbahn* doors closing and bicycle bells dinging as riders sped up the Allee. No one came to see me, not even the Kaiser, who called to say he was in Valencia drinking vermouth and guzzling mariscos with his Spanish girl Rosa. My nights endured, sleepless, unending, greeted only by a pale crust of morning that quickly extinguished into night as

January passed outside my window in a rhythmic, wholesale kind of gloom.

Still afraid to call my illness by its name, I saw no point getting a diagnosis because I knew there wasn't any antidote to the disease. None, anyway, that a medic could prescribe. No, the only place to find treatment for a sickness like mine, I realized, was the past, so in what must have been early February I clamored out from underneath Eduardo's blankets, dug through my worn bags of belongings and retrieved the small bundle of papers and personal effects I had been carrying since I left America. At the bottom of the stack of pages, pressed neatly between two folders, was a thin tan envelope that Dad had mailed to me shortly after Nana Elsa died. He told me he had discovered it buried in a mound of documents on the top shelf of her closet, wrapped inside a piece of tissue with the words written on it: *For Max.* The inside of the envelope smelled of pencil lead, cotton balls and dust. I reached in and withdrew the small stiff piece of cardboard. It was grayish yellow, almost weightless. The print had so faded that the words were barely visible. I studied the pencil marks etched in Aunt Josey's tiny hand, written in miniscule letters with the German words pressed tightly to one another. On the other side of the card, three faint words bore the address:

ALBERT EINSTEIN, U.S.A.

That this card scratched out on the tundra frozen edge of Earth had ever left Yakutsk was a miracle. That it had crossed a continent and, after that, an ocean, was more the work of some benevolent God. But that it had reached its destination at the office of Herr Professor Doktor Albert Einstein located in Princeton, New Jersey; that the Herr Professor Doktor

had faithfully passed the card to his assistant Valentin Bergmann, a former Berlin classmate of the Grunefeld sisters;
and that Herr Bergmann had tracked down among the seven
and a half million souls living in New York City one remote
Queens residence where the estranged immigrants Krumkotkin lived: This, for me, bore the stature of Myth.

I sat in Eduardo's kitchen and regained my health over the
coming weeks drinking *Hefeweizen* and consuming pouches
of Old Virginia tobacco as I read and reread the postcard
that was my inheritance. A myth, it might have been, but
one that I now held between my fingers like a key almost,
ready to unlock what unanswered questions about my family
I had not yet even asked. Families loathe themselves and love
themselves for a reason, but they don't necessarily make the
secret of their loathing known, not even to each other. And
for me the first question of loathing came down to why I,
Maximilian Krumm, had returned to this cursed city of my
ancestors in the first place.

* * *

The fact is, when Germans ask me why I'm in Berlin, I
cringe. I can't help it. It isn't that I have nothing to say to
them, it's that I don't know where to begin. I know it's a conversation starter: a simple enough, legitimate and inoffensive question. But when a German looks me up and down
and with an ironic glare asks, "Why are you here?" my heart
hears the question, *What brought you, a Jew, back to this city,
to this country, which is only creating an embarrassment for
me the German and for you the Jew?* Naturally I don't have a
readymade response so I have to think up something fresh
each time to say to them. I'm here for the past—I'm here to
exhume and eradicate and silence the unsilenceable past—
but I don't tell them that. It's too easy to make excuses in this

godless city where the rent is cheap, the art is ripe and the living is good. The ancestors of the slaughtered aren't picky, I want to tell them. Graveyards don't bother us. We'll flock just about anyplace, to Gerona and Vienna, to Russia, to Ukraine, to the Goddamned Pale of Settlement if necessary. We'll go all the way back to the Polish ghetto if someone suddenly stood up and told us it's the place to be. We'll move right back into the bloody ghetto and call the place our home.

But like it or not, the Jew in Berlin must excuse himself for simply being here. His mere presence begs further explanation; simply being here isn't enough. It's still too shocking that a Jew should just turn up and put down roots in this capital of capitals—in this inferno of his past. A Jew cannot just simply come to Berlin: He needs an alibi. Above all he needs a steel plate reinforcing his heart and his balls to ward off the spirit of disgust that his being here evokes in him. It would be intolerable for him simply to arrive with that nonchalant appeal: "Now I'll live in Berlin!" No one would understand him, least of all himself, so the Jew in Berlin hides behind one sheepish answer or another. Maybe he hasn't thought properly through the question, or perhaps he has yet to reconcile with his choice. Show me a people who have returned to the smoldering ashes of their greatest massacre and rebuilt camp, because that is precisely what we returners are doing.

The truth is that I came to Berlin and against all discomforting signs stayed living in Berlin for the same reason so many Jews are now coming to and staying and living in Berlin: because Berlin has had the madness boiled out of it. Berlin is exhausted. The Berlin that birthed creative genius and absurd impulse—the Berlin that embodied *what modern is*—is dead and gone. Gone is the tension, gone the defiance. Gone too is Joseph Roth's "strange and mournful ghetto world" on Hirtenstrasse in the former Jewish slum of Mitte, known as the Scheunenviertel, where the "the peril of the East" once clustered. Now the peril comes from the West: from New York and Los Angeles, from London, Montreal, Buenos Aires and Tel Aviv. More yids than you can count are bumbling around Berlin these days. They come as directors and musicians, journalists and painters, linguists and theorists. They arrive cloaked in the robes of businessmen, lawyers, lobbyists and poets. Others show up as teachers and translators, as guides, bakers, spouses, doctors, acrobats, digital age designers and liberal occult experimenters. Innumerable and unexplainable, these Jews are returning to Berlin as though history hadn't turned them out—as though being a Jew in Germany were the most natural thing to be. Every day they come flopping up on the banks of the Spree like a fresh batch of refugees, dragging their disappointments and dreams behind them. They come to trade ideas and to buy real estate and to sell history—above all history, because in Berlin the Jew more than any other feels the immovable weight of history like gravity pulling him down. The load cripples him almost to the point that he can't stand up straight. Once more he's being looked at, scrutinized, talked about, envied, misinterpreted, ignored and pitied and it's happening all at once. The Jew in Berlin peddles history because he has nothing left to peddle. The centuries bleed like an open sore across his back and they're written in deep creases on his brow because that is where the geography of his suffering is engraved: tattooed like a map to a country that no longer exists.

But the Jew has also come back to Berlin for a more specific reason: because it's easy to fall in with a people who are still reckoning, who are in a constant sickness-provoking state of reckoning and accounting and explaining and thus are unequipped to defend themselves against the past. I'll say it now: Germans are magnificent. They have achieved and given us magnificent things—contributions to music and science, philosophy and art, poetry and culture too abundant to name. But to be a German, what a curse! The German is so busy remembering his past that the Jew feels almost sympathy for him. At times he even finds in himself the capacity to forgive him. But the Jew doles out his forgiveness sparingly and in the other hand he holds a whip. Want to know how to silence a German, how to earn his simultaneous scorn, guilt and sometimes his respect? Tell him where your family comes from. Tell him you have returned—you have made your *Umkehr*. Tell the German: "Don't worry about today, it's your past I've come for." You can even laugh with him about it—"Yes it's true I've landed back in this city where my people's annihilation was planned and my un-existence was in the making"—because the German, despite what they say, has a rich sense of humor. He may never learn to produce it but he will almost always know how to appreciate it. The fact is the Jew isn't nearly as uncomfortable with the German as the German is uncomfortable with himself. It is the reason he welcomes you back with trembling arms: because contrition, and the disgrace of history, oblige him.

Yet when a German asks me why I'm in Berlin I cringe because it's a simple enough, legitimate and inoffensive question to which I still don't have an inoffensive answer. I'll admit, I was irrational coming to Berlin. I don't know what made me do it or what I hoped to find here. Nana Elsa said it to me herself: "Leave that place alone, Max, don't go *back there*." Perhaps Nana was right. Perhaps I had no business going *back there* to her and Aunt Josey's past; perhaps I had no business moving backward at all when I should have been moving forward. Something always smacked of the forbidden when Nana talked about *back there,* but forbidding a grandchild to know his past is like leaving a steak under the porch steps hoping the dog won't find it. The truth is, after Aunt Josey's postcard fell through oceans of improbability into my hands, I felt a cankerous desire to expose what none in my

28

family had exposed, mainly because it had not yet been discovered. Unspoken, secretive, consequential: The truth was all those things. But instead of facts all I had was a postcard. I also had something that my relatives did not have: Freedom. Lots of freedom. The freedom to go anyplace and become anything, which cannot be said for Josephine or Abram or Elsa who had a war to contend with, who had labor and concentration camps to confront and whose decisions—whose actions for chrissakes—finally meant something. Show me a war that I must fight or flee. Tell me what urgency and survival even mean. I am a disposable man living in a disposable age in which my actions, my decisions and my freedom itself are little more than symbol. What is there, after all, that a disposable man must choose from? What, more importantly, does he choose for?

I never intended to sink down roots in this godforsaken city where the only voices you hear when you step out your door in the morning are the voices of the birds and the voices of the dead. The truth is I had waited until after Nana Elsa died, at the austere age of 93, to revisit the forbidden hole of memory that she had done her utmost to prevent me falling into. I waited, I thought, out of respect. But the voices of my ancestors had been speaking to me for as long as I could remember, and not just their voices but their silences, too. My relatives were restless in their post mortem wanderings and so they pestered me. I could tell it was them because of the solitary dreams I was having where no one spoke and no one answered, no one saw me or even knew I was there, I was mute, invisible, on top of it all I was bored, extremely bored and profoundly alone with the dread that things had gone terribly wrong and would end badly. I woke up with death like the morning rotting on my lips and that is when I realized my relatives were succeeding. Abram, Elsa, Josey, I knew what they were after—they were after the *truth*—and they would harass and reduce and isolate me until I assented. Their murmurings grew louder and in my illness that February, writing on the mattress next to Eduardo's coal oven, I began hearing more than their murmurs. On one occasion I picked out a voice that was speaking to me in a sort of whisper. The voice said: *Get on with it.* Get on with what? I asked but the voice didn't answer. *Get on with it!* the voice repeated, droning the phrase again and again until it was a mantra buzzing around inside my skull. I was helpless to defend myself against it. I was tired of the nightmares. Tired of the solitude and of waiting without knowing what I was waiting for. If there was ever a moment when I was stalled and impotent and could feel the dust of time settling over my eyelids; when I needed a sign, a signal, any gust of wind to blow me back on to the pages of life so that I might discover some significance in my own, the postcard was my sign. Josephine's card was my signal.

FIVE

THEN ONE DAY THE CZAR WAS GONE

Smolensk, 1922

Abram Mikhailovich Krumkotkin was born exceedingly dark. He grew up a small boy, so dark and so small that when he was a child in the western Russian city of Smolensk, midway between Moscow and Minsk, they knew him by a single word: *Tziganok*. The Gypsy. Like other Russian boys the Gypsy played football. The Gypsy played chess. As far as I know, though, neither Russians nor gypsies were circumcised the way Abram Mikhailovich was circumcised which might help explain why his earliest schoolboy memory was the day he zipped up his trousers and could hear the other boys snickering as he left the latrine, "Hey, there goes a circumcised one!" All stories begin with memories, many of them kinder than this, and if there was a place Abram's journey truly began it was on the day his father forbade him to eat the blueberries.

It was a warm spring morning in 1916 when Mikhail Jakobovich—whose forehead by this time no longer showed signs of the horns that were once growing there—took his seven year old son to a nearby village with a heavy wicker basket balanced on his knees. The coach was crowded, the air an odorous mix of onions, earth and sweat. The train made frequent stops during which some peasants dragged their odd-shaped bundles off the train and others dragged new ones on. Two men with coarse, tobacco-stained beards were sitting next to Abram, trading in bread and candles, when a guard stopped and asked to see his father's papers.

31

"You could be a Red Army deserter or an illegal trader, who can be sure these days?" said the guard, casting a severe glance. Mikhail invited him to look inside the wicker basket that he was holding on his knees. The guard removed the lid, peered in on a mound of ripe dark blueberries and snorted as he moved to the next passenger. Before Abram could reach his hand into the basket his father's voice struck him sharply. "Don't eat the blueberries."

They got off at a station not far from Smolensk and walked until they reached a village where six wooden huts stood clustered around a dusty lane. His father pointed at the straw and mud that was stuffed in the spaces where the logs weren't fitted properly. Finally they stopped at a door where he knocked. A small man with cloudy eyes and gray side-whiskers opened it, inviting them inside. The hut was dark, damp, with a dirt floor and a clay oven at its center. Once his eyes adjusted to the light Abram noticed the walls were coated black with soot, and instead of glass a dried bull's bladder hung in the window. Abram sat in silence on a pine bench as the old man hoisted the basket on to a table. He removed the lid and plunged in his hands. His fingers dug feverishly through the blueberries, scooping out pile after pile before they reached what lay beneath: a glistening white mountain of salt. The man's eyes lit up.

"Oy Mikhail Jakobovich," he purred, "what have you brought me!"

"Enough I should think, Grisha Borisovich, to cure your meats and cabbage for a year," replied Misha, winking at his son.

Abram listened to the rousing negotiations that followed, after which the men shook hands and his father led him out of the darkness into the light carrying the basket with lard, butter and curds buried under the same blueberries.

He was eight the next summer when the fighting broke out. They were at the *dacha* in Gniezdovo. Trout were leaping from the Dnieper River and berries were bursting off their vines but Misha prohibited Abram and his younger brother Lev from walking in the forest or fishing in the river. "Vasya Victorovich had his throat slit by a band of robbers in the woods last week," he told them with knotted lips, "I'm not taking any chances." So Misha hired a Georgian to protect them. The Georgian had a thick black moustache and he wore a *cherkesska* coat that narrowed at the waist and flared at the knees. He kept cartridges in his breast pocket and tucked in his belt were two daggers that Abram and Lev watched him sharpen each morning on a whetstone in the yard. Then one afternoon the *dacha* was broken into and Misha declared, "Enough!" Dusya packed the linens, the plates, the lamps and tools and silverware, and Misha paid a peasant to haul their things by wagon back to Smolensk. It was a long, bumpy ride as Abram, sitting atop one of the mattresses, gazed into his father's eyes which were hovering like cold empty sores on his face. His father might have been staring back at Gniezdovo or he might have been looking someplace more distant than Abram or Lev or Mother could see. The past perhaps. Or the future. His father might not have been seeing anything at all for the layer of water that formed like a glass pane covering his eyes.

One week before the Red Army attacked, the Krumkotkins fled for safety in a small resort town called Eupthoria on the Black Sea coast. Abram and Lev rode in a sailboat for the first time and spent their days on the beach collecting colored stones which they saved in a wooden box labeled *Crimea 1917*. Then, when the worst of the danger was over, Misha put the family back on a train and they returned to the stench of war that was burning across the Russian nation. Abram gazed at the desperate crowds waiting in overcrowded stations. He glimpsed nervous hands clutching tickets and passengers standing immobile with faces white as chalk. Long freight cars filled with soldiers rushed past their train and when they finally reached Smolensk the streets were crowded with men waving red flags and pressing red bands to their chests as they pumped their fists into the air. Traffic stopped. Stores closed.

Then one day the Czar was gone.

Misha stood at the window as soldiers with rifles marched a column of prisoners past their home on Odegitryevskaya Street. Now they were calling it International Street and Abram listened as the children leaned from broken doorways singing:

> Down with the clergy
> Down with the rabbis
> Let's climb to heaven
> To kick out the gods!

He asked his father where the soldiers were taking the men. "On their way to firing squad," Misha whispered as they peered from behind the curtain. Misha recognized his friend, the banker Lushkov, among the condemned. Stepping back from the window he said with solemn eyes: "The men who achieved great things in Russia now have nothing, Abramchik, and the ones who had nothing have everything."

* * *

Not long after, a group of soldiers showed up one night and searched the Krumkotkins' home. They said they were looking for "counterrevolutionary materials" and when they didn't find any they took Misha away instead. Every week Abram walked with his mother, who carried a food parcel under her arm, and they stood with other families buried ankle deep in snow outside the gates of Smolensk Prison. They had no way of knowing if Misha received the packages—no way to know if he was even alive until the day, several months later, when a pale and brittle man they did not recognize came home to live with them again. Misha had a tangled beard, his cheeks were sunk into his face, his eyes yellow. His first night back he jabbered on with stories from the prison. Then two days later he caught pneumonia and lay speechless in bed. A doctor named Ivanov visited the house twice a day, and one evening Dusya approached him in her unwashed robe with hair that had been left down and uncombed for days. She looked at the doctor with imploring eyes. "You will save him, won't you Doctor?" she said, forcing a wad of bills into his hand. Ivanov issued orders that Dusya followed religiously. She fed Misha warm broth day and night. She changed his head compresses regularly and kept the stove in the bedroom lit at all hours. Over the course of weeks the light began to return to Misha's eyes and Dusya wept quiet tears as her husband regained his health.

By this time it was winter 1918 and civil war between the Bolsheviks and Mensheviks was raging in the countryside. One foggy morning a group of four Red Guard soldiers appeared at the Krumkotkins with a notice assigning them to live there. The men were fighting the counterrevolutionaries outside Smolensk and every evening they would return home dressed in long military coats and fur hats with rifles slung over their shoulders, and stomp in single file through the kitchen, the living room and into the single bedroom that used to belong to Abram and Lev. Since Misha's trade had been suspended by government decree, the family grew used to long days and nights enclosed together inside the home.

Misha would balance their slim finances or read aloud from Tolstoy while Dusya mended tattered shirts and pants, Lev worked on building a glass-needle radio set and Abram studied chess or sketched. The ruble was worthless and material of every sort was scarce. Misha turned a trunk lid into a workbench where he hammered wooden nails through scraps of leather to repair their shoes. Abram and his brother meanwhile spent afternoons scouring the city for pieces of rubber and metal that they could trade for food in the market square outside Molochov Gate. Entering the market for Abram was like inhabiting another world. He navigated the riot of animal carts and crowded stalls where angry-faced peasants shuffled around in ripped linens and *lapti* slippers, husbands bickered with wives, wives scolded husbands and everyone was out to cheat his neighbor. One morning in desperation Abram showed up at the market with a piece of rope, some towels, a spool of thread and Lev's penknife, which he exchanged for a bag of curds that the Krumkotkins devoured in a single sitting. The Civil War dragged on month after month, year after year, and even when it seemed things could not get worse, they did. In the heart of winter the family ran out of firewood. Neighbors had stolen the last stakes from the Krumkotkin fence to burn and Misha sat at the table in his winter coat shivering like it was the end of time.

Then, all of a sudden, the war was over. Boarded-up shops reopened and Misha was permitted to resume his trade. Abram watched as giant bales of flax and hemp, bound in cotton fittings, began showing up in their yard. For the first time in years he saw his father grin. "It's the work of Lenin's New Economic Policy!" Misha proclaimed with a timbre of confidence that hinted at things to come. Soon the Krumkotkins were welcoming a string of tenants into their home, part of the new spirit of Communism. First came the repairman, Dmitri, with his large hands and his constantly ill wife,

Sonya, who ate garlic as her only medication. There was the wrinkly Varvara Feodorovna, a spinster from one of the has-been landowner families, who hid her scrawny figure in long dresses that dragged on the floor behind her. Then, in the late months of 1922, a man arrived at the Krumkotkin doorstep who would forever change Abram's life.

His name was Professor Konstantin Solomonovich Buchholz and he was a scholar of German language and literature. Herr Prof. Buchholz shaved every morning, smoked cigars and wore a derby hat with a tailored jacket that he brushed meticulously—a measure that earned him laughter in the streets of Smolensk where men still trudged around in soldiers' overcoats smoking dark *majorka* shwag wrapped in newspaper. Yes, Buchholz was an oddity in the city but Misha knew a gift when he saw one. He lowered Konstantin Solomonovich's rent by half in exchange for daily German lessons for his teenage son. Within two years Abram was reading Goethe, reciting Heine and translating Börne. By sixteen his essays on Nietzsche and Marx demonstrated not only a facility with the German language but, more importantly in Prof. Buchholz's appraisal, they showed an understanding of the richness of German expression and German thought. It is doubtful Abram Mikhailovich had any idea then of the impact the professor would have on his future—namely, that their tedious long hours of German would one day provide Abram the opportunity to slip silently, clandestinely, through a fissure-like crack in the Soviet empire and embark on a new destiny in the West. For Misha, of course, who had never made it out of Russia—who had sinned in murder and, as a result, failed to reach that glittering opportune patch of earth known as Abroad—the fate of his firstborn was clear: When the moment arrived, when chance became probability, it was decided that Abram would go to Berlin, to that blazing torch of civilization which glowed only a train ride away.

SIX

CHAGALL'S

I finally escaped the apartment—and, it seemed, along with it, my illness—on a Tuesday night in late February. It was after one of those fresh, clean mid-winter freezes when ice still clings in the air and your breath pours out thick as a cloud. I'd got to Café Chagall before the others so I rolled a cigarette and stood out on the handsome slope of Senefelder Platz watching the early night crowds pass.

Berlin's always lit on Tuesdays. It's lit on Sundays and Mondays, too, but those are more for the dining crews. On Wednesday the drinks are pouring like it's the weekend and by Thursday your home-by-morning nights begin in earnest. But Tuesdays are different. Tuesdays are for the regulars. You know the cliché about Germany: that life there runs with regularity and almost clock-like consistency. Germans are addicted to consistency the way Italians are addicted to parmigiano and when it comes to exercising that consistency, nothing is more regular than Tuesday drinking nights known as the *Stammtisch*. The *Stammtisch* is little more than a mid-week excuse to swill liters of *Hefe* with your professional or otherwise "exclusive" group of comrades. There are *Stammtischen* for academics and *Stammtischen* for city councilmen, for opera singers, librarians, artists and about any other group with a shared interest. There are even *Stammtischen* for Berlin Jews although I never enjoyed those meetings because all those people ever talked about was being Jews. Fortunately my *Stammtisch* had nothing to do with being anything but what Easy Wayne and Alan and Robert and myself had in common, that is, our love of drink and smoke and the company of disposable men.

As I stood out on the Platz waiting for others to arrive, I admired the bicyclists pumping in a steady procession up Schönhauser Allee. You can learn a lot about the Berg—Prenzlauer Berg—by standing out there and watching Bergers pedal uphill home from work in the cold darkness. First you notice an immediate difference between the sexes. The women on their bicycles look exhausted but their faces are invigorated. Their bikes are mostly mounted with children's seats, sometimes with the little blond beasts inside them, and you can see in those glowing maternal eyes what the women are looking forward to once they get home. Something radiates in their satisfied expression; you see fulfillment, affirmation and realization in the exuberant gazes and exercising legs of all those Prenzlauer Berg women.

The men on their bicycles however tell a different story. Naturally they look grimmer. This is because the Prenzlauer Berg men are peddling without any real desire to get where they are going. Their emotionless faces give them away: Their studies have been too sedate, their jobs too stressful, their lives too routine and on top of that their evening has little to offer. Aged roughly twenty six to forty three, these quashed fellows represent the core of the Berg and embody the new sluggish and unexcitable middle class of Germans who have overrun the place. A good many of these men are lost in the labyrinthine pursuit of a German university degree. They are aging after their time, acutely aware that youth is expiring noiselessly before their eyes. Others meanwhile have managed to leap life's greatest hurdle and are now considered the Papas of the Berg. These men form the distinguished and, in a sense, the crème cadre of this bobo heaven. Their children are spreading like wildfire through the Berg (they say more babies are born per Prenzlauer Berg block than anyplace in Europe, three-quarters of them conceived on Ikea bed frames). The fathers also sometimes ride with baby seats mounted on their bikes though more often you see these Prenzlauer Berg men pushing strollers. Their primary purpose now is to handle a baby basket on wheels. Walk through the Berg and you'll collide with a man steering a four-wheeled buggy at every block. The carriages clog the sidewalks; they're an annoyance to childless people everywhere and especially to the men who are pushing them. These fathers' eyes however have stopped protesting and are now locked in a cold blue foggy fixture on their faces. The fathers see their futures squirming on the seats in front of them while their wives, or more often their girlfriends, walk beside them looking happier. Naturally they're happier. The women in the Berg are precisely where they want to be: They have arrived. Life has offered up a career that excites them and a culture that distracts them and it has even handed them a Prenzlauer Berg man with whom they have born a child. Now they are raising that child in the coziest neighborhood of the most desirable city in the West so what, precisely, is there to be unhappy about? There is no violence in the Berg. There is no crime in the Berg. There isn't even any noise in the Berg—no arguments or music or even car horns—in fact no disturbances of any kind, which is why these young Fraus breathe with a relieved sense of completion. They can't conceive of a single threat least of all the threat that their Prenzlauer Berg man pushing the *Kinderwagen* will one day awaken and revolt. Jumping ship for the fathers of the Berg is not an option. They have been too meticulous and methodical building up this life of ease to barter it all away now. Sure, life in nirvana gets dull sometimes. But mark my words: The Prenzlauer Berg man will not flee. He has made his deal, and he has no parachute, no other, better or more imaginable plan at his disposal.

* * *

Woyzeck was working the bar when I entered. "Max!" he shouted and threw a scarred right arm around my neck. Woyzeck got chewed up by his brother-in-law's pit bull the previous Christmas in Poland, but the musculature in his forearm was growing back. Woyzeck was sturdy. He had a broad pale face, tiny blue eyes and a sharp nose: your model Pole. He was living black without papers like a lot of Poles in Berlin and a lot of Poles everywhere. Some days he earned cash building stage sets or driving a tour bus but mostly he stayed home drinking. The only reason he said he bothered working evenings at Chagall's was to escape his girlfriend Glasha who bitched at him to no end.

"Where have you been, Max? Here, I've been saving it for you all this time," he said, handing me a shot of Grasovka. "L'chaim my friend. You must call me one of these days. We should talk."

"We should, Woyzeck," I said, and I meant it. Our glasses touched. We drank.

"I have so much time on my hands, you know how it is," Woyzeck went on. "They rarely call me in for work so I sit in the apartment and try to read as I listen to Glasha getting hysterical. Right now I am reading a book about Iranian oil industry."

"You never stop."

"Yeah but I never go either," Woyzeck said with a grin as his eyes crinkled into wee nutshells above his nose. "Just tell me when you're free, we'll talk."

"I will. Any of the guys here?"

"Alan came in but he is all. What will you have?"

I ordered a dark Krušovice then stepped through the maze of crowded tables, candles and voices occupying the front room and followed the narrow green corridor to the back.

Alan, seated alone in a corner, was pecking on his phone as a pint of Jever perspired on the table.

"Writing your Uzbeki?" I said, sliding out a chair opposite him.

"She's Tajiki," Alan said without looking up. "From Tajikistan."

"Yeah. Tajikistan."

"I'm seeing if she wants to come over and blow me later," he said.

"No kidding."

"All we've been doing is fucking, that's all we do, Max. She doesn't want anything more. It's incredible."

"That is."

"But I have to say I'm actually starting to get bored, I mean, there's nothing really for us to talk about. She comes over, blows me for a bit, I fuck her, fuck her some more, then she leaves."

Woyzeck arrived with my Krušovice. I took a sip, pulled out my pouch and started to roll one.

"That's how you want it though, isn't it?"

"Pretty much, but it still gets boring. Now she's asking me to take her out, see a movie, go to a restaurant, that kind of shit."

"Why don't you?"

"Not interested," Alan said with a belch. "Big waste of time. What are we going to do, go out, have dinner, watch a film, then talk? No. We're going to go back to my place and fuck so what's the point of dinner and a movie? It's boring, man, she's only twenty one, nice girl, serious about her studies. But no."

Just then Alan's phone quacked. He picked it up, stared impatiently at the text, took a sip of his Jever and returned to pecking. Alan was pale, slightly overweight, with big restless brown eyes that refracted tiredly through his wire-frame glasses. He wasn't unattractive; on the contrary, his features had a boyish almost tenderness that contrasted with the sour man inside him. There was a sarcastic look Alan couldn't wipe off his face, a kind of constant discomfort suffusing his Ashkenazic brow. After perving all night at 8 Millimeter and White Trash where he tried to take home Asians half his age, Alan would spend the day locked in his studio apartment overlooking Falkplatz, on the edge of Mauerpark, hammering the jigsaw of his unnaturally flowing prose into place. He hounded the editors back home who sometimes published his work but often didn't, and never enough to make him happy. He was an anxious bachelor rolling on forty with a temperament that bordered on despair. But Alan also had a soft vulnerability and unrepentant honesty that drew you to him. Once in a while he would erupt in laughter, a cackling giddy contagious kind of laugh that got the whole place going. There was a pot-bellied sort of wisdom to the man, you just had to know where to look.

"And the London job," I said, "how's it going?"

"That rag? I stopped writing for them months ago. The British press is a joke, Max, all they want are Nazi and sex stories, that's it, like the headline they ran a few weeks back—"RECENT DISCOVERY FINDS HITLER WAS FLAT-ULENT"—that kind of shit, or they'll take some brief about a Bavarian farmer whose sister killed him with an axe after he molested her daughter. No culture, no politics, no news. The Brits still think it's Third Reich porn season over here and—"

"There he is," I said, glad to interrupt Alan mid-rant and extend a hand to Easy Wayne.

"What's up brothers! Alright alright, everything cool? You cats all cool alright," said Wayne, towering over the table.

"Easy Wayne, how goes?" said Alan, returning to his phone.

"Good good, actually I'm doing pretty alright I gotta say.

43

How about you, Max, things cool you good everything cool?"

"I'm good."

"Good good, glad to hear you cats are doing alright," he said and slumped down in a chair next to Alan.

"Nice to see you again Wayne!" shouted Woyzeck, who had snuck up on us and now stood there beaming like a bright potato. "What's it been, a whole fucking week and you don't even greet me when you come in the door?"

"Oh man how you doing Woyzeck, sorry about that bro yeah everything's cool and I'll tell you what, how about bringing me one of those big dark mothers right there like he's having," Wayne said, nodding at my beer. When Woyzeck disappeared Wayne breathed a heavy sigh, pulled out his pouch and leaned back deep in his seat with his long legs stretched out, then started to roll one. Easy Wayne had that easy way about him. He had a thick long brown mane of hair like a lion's that arched high off his forehead and dropped in a majestic wave down his neck. The moment you saw Wayne you knew his hair was his best quality. It had to be. God doesn't endow men with hair like Wayne's and a whole lot else. But He threw Wayne some television good looks while He was at it and Wayne smiled because he knew that it was good. He had a wide full face and a tomorrow-be-damned twinkle in his eyes like he just stepped off a motorcycle after gunning it across open desert. The amazing thing was that Wayne wasn't gunning anywhere. He had no intention to gun anything and goddamn if he wasn't thirty six and still a translator of sterile texts living in an unsterile town. Easy Wayne was twelve years in Berlin and a fixture in the Berg. Like those big buck antlers you see hanging in Thuringian restaurants, Wayne was damn fine to look at and he wasn't going anywhere. I envied him because it seemed there wasn't a thing in the world he needed or wanted to do; nothing, it appeared, that he hoped or imagined to one day accomplish.

Easy Wayne had a strong Midwestern heart that was absent of ambition and it was alright by him.

He lit his smoke and blew out a thick plume. "Where's our other cat?" he said. "Robert coming?"

"He's on his way," said Alan.

Woyzeck arrived with Wayne's Kršovice and after he took a swallow he snorted, "Goddamn, is this the weekend boys because it feels like the weekend! I don't know about you dudes but I gotta say I'm feeling pretty good, pretty fucking alright and about ready to rip a fat one, what do you cats say to ripping a fattie?"

"Start us off," said Alan, looking glum as he stared into his phone.

"I mean shit," said Wayne, fiddling in his pouch as he searched for the hash stud mixed with his tobacco. "I just came from my Romanian's place and all, remember I told you about that hottie I'm seeing down on Karl Marx Allee, so I'm feeling a little, you know, kind of a little like I'm needing some kickback time with the boys is all."

"Your Romanian? Where do you find these women?"

"Everywhere, Max, they're goddamn everywhere and man this girl she knows what's up. I go over there and I'm like, 'Yeah you know what's up baby,' and she's like, 'Yeah you know what's up,' and we just get to fucking and that's it. Max dude you gotta get your ass back out there. It's been what, half a year since Lotte and you're still drying on the vine? Too many hot damn women in this town to be wasting like that, bro, you got to get your shit in action know what I mean."

"Yeah," I said as Wayne flicked the lighter and heated the hash, crumbling bits of it into his palm. Just then Woyzeck swooped in with three fresh rounds and he also replaced the candle that was burning low on the table—burning like we in our weekly *Stammtisch* mutterings were burning as our shadows flickered across the low wood ceiling at Chagall's. That back room was our dungeon, our medieval chamber. There were bricks showing through the cracks of the chipped plaster and old warped sketches of coastlines hung at crooked angles on the wall. An ancient yellowed map of the world, punctured and peeling, was tacked above the fireplace that was never lit but oh we got lit, yes, we got lit in the back room at Chagall's, a place so charred it looked like the inside of a chimney with black streaks and smudge marks running up the walls, and yeah it was seedy, yeah it was claustrophobic with the uneven floorboards that made you feel like you were rocking and maybe like you were sinking in the belly of some great death ship, but it was our death ship and our wooden table and wooden chairs, and we basked in the glow of the neon "Restaurant" sign that hummed and glared through the back room and made us feel at Chagall's like somehow we were home.

"I mean shit," Wayne continued, "what are you Max, thirty two, thirty three, you're single, you got rid of that German running your ass around—"

"She got rid of him," croaked Alan.

"Whatever dude! The point is you gotta get out there because you're not getting any younger but the chicks are and there's nothing like springtime in Berlin."

"Ohhhh-yeeeah," belched Alan again, picking up his phone to peck another message. There was silence then as Wayne lit the bifter and took a few puffs. He was about to pass it my way when a voice like a foghorn bellowed from behind.

"Looks like ahm jost in time!" Robert slung his guitar off his shoulder.

"Just in time, my man, just in time—y'all this cat can smell it!" Wayne held out the joint to Robert by way of a handshake.

"Yeh Wayne ah think we could do with some o' that. Hey alright then fellas how you doin yeh? Things are sound, sound," said Robert. He set his guitar on the floor beside the table and took off his coat. Alan's phone quacked, this time from his pocket. "Haha, Alan's on about the Chinese mistress again is he?" Robert squinted as he took a drag and sat down next to me.

"You been playing or what?" said Wayne.

Robert's heavy green eyes pinched up again as he took another draw on Wayne's bifter before passing it to Alan. He shook his head. "Ol day long yeh, hey Wayne can ah jost get a nip of your baccy, ah din't have time to pick some op."

"Dude." Wayne pushed the pouch across the table and Robert started to roll one. Robert had a bright silver hood of hair and a face like a barnacle, gnarled and unpolished. His life was something like a barnacle's, too, stuck and hard and weathering the years, barely hanging on as oceans of predicaments crashed around him causing him to spit out philosophical pebbles from time to time. Robert had fled smalltown Yorkshire and his words had the musical sound of another century. I remember when things started getting rough for me and Lotte, Robert said, "Why'ont you jost get on with it an marry er?" "Marry her?" I said. "Yeh what you fussin bout then, she's a good Kraut that frau, you can handle er." Robert sold me on Lotte the way he could sell you on anything: convinced, innocent, all-knowing. He spent his days trolling Berlin with a guitar on his back and a loose hobo's gait: feet splayed, legs kicking outward like Charlie Chaplain in old loose jeans that swallowed up his canvas shoes. Robert took handouts everywhere he went. Tea. Biscuits. A metro card. A shot of whiskey. A shirt. A hat. A book. Robert took whatever you had to give him and all day long he trolled with that battered twang guitar stuffed in its ragged case. He took it out to play for an hour in his pupils' apartments where he'd drink their beer and smoke their weed and leave with a twenty euro note stuffed in his coat pocket. Robert was skinned: He didn't have a dime. All he had was that thick syrupy Yorkshire accent that forced you to love him and forced you to positively listen to what he was saying as he winked and nodded and spoke with a deep set honest glimmer in his eye.

"So dudes hear me out," said Wayne, leaning suddenly close in over the table like he was about to leak a state secret. We all sat listening but the truth is no one expected to hear a thing because once Easy Wayne got to smoking he got to babbling. He'd babble about all kinds of things, crackpot notions concerning genetics and Darwinism and the fixed obvious qualities of the sexes. Wayne had every kind of unresolved theory rattling around in that handsome oversized skull of his, from biological inevitability to libido conspiracy and once the bifters got rolling and the night ascended there was no stopping him. You couldn't argue and you couldn't reason with Wayne because if you did he'd throw one of his bio-psycho-physio-gibberish acts and tell you how it all goes back to the male and the female gene. Intellectually it was all he cared about: arguing for Darwin and against God and proclaiming that men and women were put on Earth to accomplish fundamentally different goals and those genetically programmed goals—having children and making a secure home for women, spreading semen as widely and eternally as possible for men—dictated our every action down to the most minute and mundane such as whether or whether not to roll another bifter. Easy Wayne spoke with dogma and conviction and he was intransigent in his beliefs, but nonetheless when his face folded into that eager crescent moon and the wave of his mane swept you up in its leonine grace, you couldn't help but listen. "What do you fellas say to a little trip?" he said finally.

"What kind of trip?" said Alan.

"Bike trip. A few days out in the open air."

"Ahm op for it!" said Robert who was always op for anything.

"Where would we go?" I said.

"How about Poland?" said Robert.

"Exactly, some shit like Poland!" said Wayne, and that got my mind turning.

"What's in Poland?" said Alan.

"Lots of rivers and forests ah reckon," said Robert, who started to roll one.

"We just fill the saddle bags with gear and we fucking go, say early June, what do you cats say?"

"Be good to blow away the cobwebs yeh."

"I've got stories to file," said Alan.

"You always got stories to file, Alan, what the fuck! We're talking about a long weekend."

"Poland," I meditated on the word. "Any idea where to?"

"Anyplace, man, doesn't matter."

"Yeh ah reckon if we jost start aiming someplace we'll have a good laugh. Ah could do with a trip."

"I bet we get us some righteous summer days in the east," Wayne continued, and as he spoke I dipped my face into my mug thinking one thought only: the postcard. There was the story I knew but also the one I didn't know, about Abram and Elsa and Josephine and what exactly happened *back there* that I didn't understand. I knew I needed to *get on with it*, to follow the trail back to where the story began—the story that my family had not ever fully explained nor in good faith revealed to their only grandson. Contrary to Nana Elsa's command, I realized that back *was* my way forward. It was the only possible direction I could go.

"Max, what are you thinking?"

"East sounds good."

"Alan?"

"My stories—"

"Fuck your stories, man! Those cocksuckers at Time or the Telegraph or wherever can wait. Maybe you can even write something about the trip," Wayne spat, giving Alan a cockeyed stare.

There was silence. Robert lit a cig and Wayne started to roll one. I did too. Alan's phone quacked. He looked down at it.

"Says she can't make it over tonight, says 'Asshole when are you going to take me out?'"

"Who's that your Chinese girl again?" Robert laughed.

Alan shrugged in defeat. He took out a rolling paper and pinched in some tobacco along with a thumb of weed from his pouch. Our cigarettes burned, our glasses emptied and something about us expiring there felt like hell but it felt sublime, too. Just then a crew of Balkan gypsies fired up their accordion, horn and fiddle out on the street, and a few moments later Woyzeck appeared balancing a tray of five beers and five shot glasses brimming with clear fluid.

"Guys tell me if I am wrong," he said, "but I have not yet heard you make a toast this evening so I came to help you out."

We each seized a glass from the tray. Wayne's left eye was dodging. It always drifted to the side when he drank and now he fixed his simian gaze on Alan as the words escaped, low and threatening like an ultimatum:

"You in?"

Alan, morose, stared at the candle flickering on the table. "Yeah I'm in."

"To Poland!" Wayne roared.

"To Poland!" we echoed and each drained his glass, all except for Woyzeck who stood paralyzed with his tiny blue eyes opened wide and his drinking hand upraised.

"To Poland? Guys, I am honored!" he said. "This may be the first and last time I hear two Jews drink to Poland, so tell me, what can I do but drink as well."

SEVEN

THE BOHEMIANS

Prague, 1938

Something you have to understand about my grandfather Abram, long before he was cuckolded, before the war drove him and Elsa off the Old Continent and before Devlovsky that son of a bitch ever came on the scene, was the plight that pushed him West to begin with: his unmet desire to be educated.

An education in 1920s Russia, you see, was closed to yids like Abram Mikhailovich. The only applicants from his class who were accepted at Smolensk University came from parents of one of three backgrounds: proletariat, peasant or the State. Abram's father Mikhail was none of these: He was a bourgeois capitalist Jew and in those days there wasn't a creature more loathed on the Russian earth. Three times Abram passed the entrance exam and three times they rejected him. As a child he'd dreamed of acting. He hoped to study literature and philosophy and art. Perhaps he would become a painter since the thing he loved most was to draw. But week after week, month after month, Abram's prospect of an education waned and it wasn't until a 1928 summer family trip to the spas at Druskininkai, on the Nemunas River southwest of Vilna, that Abram met the second man who would quietly but profoundly shape his life.

He was a tiny fellow who went by the name Silzovsky. Like Misha, Silzovsky was a businessman. He wore heavy round glasses through which his pupils appeared like microscopic dots. Only a few damp gray whiskers of hair stuck to his scalp. Also like Misha, Silzovsky had been prescribed two weeks at the curative baths of Druskininkai in order that the inhalation of vapors might ease his emphysema. The men, both speaking with a shortness of breath, became fast friends. They sat for hours in the steam discussing commerce, politics and art, and though Abram would listen to their conversations he remained too tentative to join them. Then one afternoon Misha left the spa early and Abram found himself seated alone across from Silzovsky whose voice cut through the dense air:

"Mikhail Jacobovich tells me you like to draw."

"I want to be an artist," replied Abram.

"What is it you like to draw?" Silzovsky said. "Or I should say, what fascinates you most?"

"People. I like drawing people."

"And buildings, what about those?" Silzovsky pressed him. "And streets and towns? Have you ever tried drawing them as well?"

"No," said Abram, studying Silzovsky's grainy outline through the mist. Some minutes passed in silence. Abram could sense that the little man was thinking; ideas and formulations were brewing inside the small bald head as it perspired with vapor. Finally Silzovsky said:

"Your father tells me you speak German, is that correct?"

"Yes."

"He also tells me the Russian universities are closed to you."

"Yes."

"Then here is an idea, Abram Mikhailovich." Silzovsky leaned in and lowered his voice almost to a whisper. "Leave Russia. Go to Berlin. There you can study to become an architect."

An architect? Abram was dumbfounded. He considered architecture dry and precise; the mere mention of the word bored him. He was an artist, after all! But Silsovsky, who was a step ahead of his audience, continued.

"It is the next best thing to art and it is a respected profession. Just think, Abram Mikhailovich, once you are an architect, you can draw anything you like."

And with that Silsovsky stood up, pressed a damp towel to his face and left the room. Later that night Abram discussed the idea with his parents, and Misha beamed with pride. So it was decided.

"Now your life will have form," he told his son, who only partly understood what he had meant.

A few weeks after the Krumkotkins returned to Smolensk, two of Misha's so-called "influential friends" visited the house and began to make arrangements. Misha paid the family physician Ivanov a princely sum of 6,000 rubles to diagnose Abram with a rare abnormality of the heart, a condition that required him to seek "treatment" abroad. The family waited patiently for news from Moscow. Two months passed. Five months. Then, shortly after the new year, Abram's passport arrived. The family celebrated with slivovic and invited over neighbors: Their boy was going West! And on a late January night in 1929, dressed in the expensive winter coat and fur hat that his mother had bought as parting gifts, Abram boarded a train which clanked across the icy Russian expanse, making stops in Minsk and Warsaw before it ground to a halt two full days later at the Westbahnhof station in Berlin.

Now isn't the time nor is there any special need to tell in detail of the life Abram Mikhailovich fashioned for himself over the next four years in the German capital. Of his only somewhat disciplined architecture studies at the Technische Hochschule in Charlottenburg. Or the barely furnished garret that he rented for 65 Deutschmarks on Fasanenstrasse, a few blocks off the Ku'damm. Or even of the frequent and solitary visits he made to the Kaiser Friedrich Museum in Mitte where, on a blustery fall afternoon, after standing side by side for many minutes admiring the same small portrait by Rembrandt, Abram introduced himself to the dark-eyed woman with glowing auburn hair and strikingly genteel features who called herself Elsa Grunefeld. No, we won't go into the romance that Abram and Elsa pursued either because that, too, is not our story. It is what happened *after* the spark was lit between them that I want to tell you about. After Abram heard the heavy marching cadence of the Hitler Youth as they made their formal first appearance in the downtown streets. After he attended a much-publicized "meeting" in the Sport Palace where thousands of men and women roared as their eyes fixed on the angular, small-headed man called Goebbels whose words of hatred stirred the voice of the new century. After the Brownshirts and the Storm Columns with their jackboots stomping the pavement outside his garret grew louder, and the gangs prowling around his doorstep at night grew more threatening. It was after Hitler assumed the German chancellorship and the Reichstag caught fire, after and only after all of that, once instinct had submerged hope, that Abram and Elsa did what it was somehow in their bones to do.

They fled.

* * *

In the summer of 1933 the couple married. Abram had spent the spring rushing applications to architecture schools across Europe—Switzerland, Sweden, Czechoslovakia—and when only the last one sent to Charles University responded favorably, they packed their bags and rode the crowded train to Prague. The venomous air of Berlin dissipated behind them and within days they had rented a flat in Prague's

Russian quarter of Dejvicka, only a few steps from Pushkin Square. Elsa enrolled at the German Medical Faculty and was generously subsidized by her father, Anton Grunefeld, who had earlier left Berlin with Elsa's sister and invalid brother to settle in their mother's home city of Kovno, Lithuania, where he ran an electrical goods store. The store provided Anton with adequate income to send his daughter a stipend, mailed faithfully each month, which allowed Elsa and Abram to live comfortably in the Czechoslovakian capital. So comfortably, in fact, that they began to entertain a social life unlike any they had imagined or experienced before.

You have to remember that Prague in the thirties, like every place in Europe, was crawling with the poor. Poverty lay just outside the Krumkotkins' doorstep. It hovered vacant-eyed on streets corners. Hands in pockets. Mouths hungry. Hundreds of them, thousands of them. The *Arbeitslosen* stood in the ruins of depression and amid the atmosphere of need, Abram and Elsa recognized their own good fortune by delivering some of it upon others. No sooner did Elsa make contact with the Young Communist League than the bohemians of Prague began showing up at their door. First came the poets and painters. Then the unemployed doctors, the students and political refugees. Finally there were starving half-crazed riffraff of every kind entering their home. Due to their relative largesse, the Krumkotkin residence overnight became a salon where men who owned nothing but their thoughts would come to discourse—to denounce Nazism and anti-Semitism and militarism and nationalism, to praise Trotsky or laud expressionism or dispute Freud, all the while angling for a piece of ham and waiting for a fresh drop of wine to fill their cups. Abram and Elsa welcomed the impoverished and the verbose, the philosophers and mavericks and penniless dissidents some of them so poor they wore suits made out of wood pulp. The sessions were boisterous, smoky and long, often ranging into the early morning hours as men and women sat curled up together on cushions sipping coffee and staring out of red nocturnal eyes. Friendships unfolded, love affairs ignited. They even ignited for Elsa whose communal spirit became less discreet. For her the party never ended at the residence but rather only seemed to begin. Elsa took to staying out very late, coming home in the dead hours before dawn. Some nights she did not return at all.

At first Abram tore himself with jealousy though he tried to play along. "And have you slept with any of them?" he stammered as his wife slipped in the door one morning around breakfast time.

"With those dirty men?" Elsa howled with laughter. "All they want is *Kameradschaft*," and she considered the discussion closed. Never mind that she and Abram had stopped sleeping together on all but the rarest occasions. Never mind too that she went in for frequent "checkups" with her Communist doctor friends among whom abortions were all the rage. How and when Abram first got cuckolded, by which "comrade," will never be known and anyway it does not matter much. The truth is there were men too numerous to count who were sniffing around his wife in those days and perhaps that is why Abram, groomed by the experience that befell his father, ceded dutifully to the illness. It began with a gnawing groinal discomfort which forced him to shift constantly on his feet to relieve the pain. The sickness then struck harder, sending him to bed for several weeks. He was attacked by nausea and cold. For a time he lost consciousness, sweating, shivering, barely clinging to life. Then all at once the illness passed. Abram regained his strength, resumed his architecture studies and one afternoon went out to meet a colleague, Felix, at their favorite tavern in the Small Town. They were looking out across the Vltava River and after their Pernods arrived his mate leveled him with a gaze. "Abram, when I see the way that you and Elsa laugh together, I think one of two things," said Felix. "Either you are the happiest couple in the world or you are the most miserable." Abram nodded, returning his friend's merciless honesty with silence.

As life renewed its routine, Abram immersed himself in studies. He spent fourteen-hour days at the drafting board applying the T-square, compass, ruler and other accouterments that helped make order of the disorderly world around him. By 1935 Hitler had wiped out the Versailles Treaty and formed a conscript army, defying the Western powers and reawakening the gods of war. Abram read in disbelief about the Nuremberg Laws and was aghast when Germany moved into Austria with Nazi mobs marching up Kärntnerstrasse. The *Anschluss* happened fast; within a week Vienna's Jews were down on their hands and knees, doctors, lawyers, merchants and rabbis all scrubbing the sidewalks and toilets with their *tefillin*. He wondered when the same might happen to them in Prague.

Then, on a warm clear August morning in 1936, a letter arrived from Kovno. Dispatched from the office of Anton Isaakovich Grunefeld, it announced the impending arrival of Elsa's sister in Prague. "Business is thriving, my ties continue to grow with military and private contractors," Grunefeld wrote to his daughter. "But Kovno is no place for Josephine to pursue her studies so I have arranged for your sister's enrollment alongside yours at the German Medical Faculty in Prague. She is on her way and will begin classes next month." Elsa tossed aside the letter in rage and stood up. "How dare Father saddle me with my little sister! Does he think we're still in Gymnasium? I won't have her here," she said. But she needed the stipend. Elsa could not refuse her father. And one week later, a nineteen-year-old girl with delicate cheeks and a round, boyish face knocked at the door, which Abram opened while holding a bottle of Moravian wine to celebrate.

Abram saw the immediate resemblance between the sisters: the anxious, hesitant expression around the lips, the heightened Berlin air of mannerisms. But Josephine struck him as somehow more graceful, with quieter charm and a less sharply challenging brow than his wife. Josey spoke in hoarse rapid whispers and when she laughed she threw her head back revealing the contours of a neck so pale and soft it looked as though it had never been touched. Abram was smitten. The two began to meet for coffee under the tall glass windows at Café Slavia, trading glances as the slow-moving Vltava rolled past. Abram would sketch while Josephine talked of life in Kovno. She told Abram about her work assisting her father's business and taking care of her sick brother Evgeny, whom she called "Bubi". Josey rarely took out her books but instead occupied herself with a mirror, applying layers of mascara and rouge like a woman who knows that she is only borrowing beauty and must one day give it back. Abram meanwhile was struggling to complete a department store design for one Professor Mandl. Mandl wanted his students to be modern: smooth facades, flat roofs, lots of glass. But feeling now emboldened by the delightful creature seated opposite him, Abram made a courageous break: He gave his building a pitched roof, small windows and a brick façade. Rebellion stirred in him as his sister-in-law awakened the thing that Abram had tried with his greatest strength to resist—desire. He succeeded through the remainder of the school term, and even into the next. But as Elsa pursued her many friendships and debauched courtships, Abram's heart grew closer with Josephine's. Their hours became more joined, their emotions more intimate. Then one morning in September 1938, what Abram believed could never happen did.

Elsa had left early for the German faculty and Abram decided to skip class and spend the day drafting in his study. He put a pot of coffee on the stove and Josephine, who was lingering getting out the door, stayed to share it with him. As a rule Abram never drank coffee while he worked, so he sat down on the couch with his cup and saucer and began thumbing through the latest issue of *The Torch*. He was chuckling at one of Karl Krauss's columns, a parody of the night Hitler's storm troopers got lost in a Viennese opera house. Abram's glee ripened into laughter punctuated by a cry, "Hah-hah!" Sitting on the sofa seat opposite him, Josephine said:

"You have a darling laugh, Abram Mikhailovich, one of the sweetest laughters I have ever heard."

"Don't tease, Josey," Abram said, shooting a pair of smiling eyes over the magazine.

"I'm not teasing. There is a gentle trill in your voice, Abram Mikhailovich, something I have fallen in love with, I think."

At the sound of the word Abram felt a shiver down his neck. Josephine wore a thin burgundy sweater and a floral shawl hung loosely around her shoulders. She reached down just then to scratch her left knee, tugging lightly at her skirt, then reclined into the sofa seat and stared at Abram from behind two crossed legs. Abram felt a heavy sweat break out across his forehead and hid his face behind the journal. Sunlight was pouring through the large front windows of the apartment which now felt to him like a furnace. Finally Josephine said:

"Abram Mikhailovich, do you find me more attractive than my sister?" She brushed the hair from her eyes. Another tickle ran through Abram as the pages fluttered in his hand.

"I cannot compare you to Elsa," he said in a rushed and angry tone. "You're such—oh you're different women, that's all!" Abram threw the journal aside, stood up and walked to his drafting board. He picked up a pencil and began to sketch. Abram's hand dashed across the board, producing lines that fused themselves in tight, chaotic symmetry. He had a sudden idea that required urgent completion: a vision working its way through him which grew frenzied as his fingers exerted more pressure. The frantic pace of his drawing overtook him. Then, in an instant he felt two hands clasp his waist and smelled Josephine's perfumed breath, warm like flowers, as she whispered in his ear:

"Come with me, Abram."

Abram paused, unable to move or think. Whiteness like a cloud filled his eyes. Then he dropped his pencil, spun around and kissed Josephine with ravenous appetite as her fingers groped at his buckle. He picked her up effortlessly and set her on the drafting table. Josephine wrapped her legs around his waist as his hands pushed up her skirt to massage her thin thighs. Josephine's head fell back. She closed her eyes and released a melody of groans while assorted pencils and erasers and metal objects fell off the drafting board with a clatter. Abram urged himself inside her, rapid, scalding. He failed to control himself and in under a minute his eyelids sweetened. The violent heaves ceased. Abram collapsed on top of Josephine, smothering her in his breath as their bodies lay suspended on the drafting board like actors frozen in a play that has just ended and who are waiting for the curtain to fall.

"You are a fine man, Abram Mikhailovich," Josephine said, cradling his head. "You have answered my question. But why, my dear Abramchik, did you ever fall in love with that sister of mine?" Abram laughed. It was a short, manic sort of laugh. Then he stood up, lifted Josephine off the drafting board and, with his shirt still unbuttoned, rushed out of the flat.

Two weeks later Hitler invaded the Sudetenland, annexing and occupying Czechoslovakia's German-speaking regions of the north and west. Abram, Elsa and Josephine gathered in the living room almost too shocked to speak. There was little consensus on what to do next. Elsa was for fleeing west via Switzerland in an attempt to reach London. But Josephine refused to abandon their father and brother in Kovno. "If there is a war coming I must return and get them out!" she demanded. Abram was less decisive. He saw no way of returning to his parents in Russia where he would be jailed, or worse, for his years living in the West. He couldn't stay put either, despite not completing his studies. Hitler's ambitions were clear: He would take the continent and no one could stop him. Abram agreed with Elsa not because he was still committed to loving her but because they needed one another in order to survive. With storm clouds gathering over Europe they began making preparations to leave and what occurred that morning between Abram and Josephine was never spoken of again.

EIGHT

MEDIA AUXILIARY

Now it's true that I am a sick and disposable man but I'll tell you: Sickness is a symptom of our age. It's not just me who's sick. We're all sick. Either that or we've been sick or we have the sickness coming to us, and no one is sicker than the disposable man for the simple reason that his sickness is himself. His malaise stares back at him in the mirror each day and there isn't a cure in sight. Ask the Kaiser and he'll tell you: The disposable man is useless because he either hasn't found his use or he's been used up. Now the Kaiser he's worked himself into a frenzy over all this and frankly I'm worried about him though the one I'm more worried about is me, understand, because my nerves are all stitched up inside and my esophageal tract has holes in it, though none of this is new. The truth is that my bellicose relationship with my gut goes back all the way to the time when I was five years old and my anus popped out of me.

It happened on a visit to Aunt Josey's, in Los Altos, California, where she moved after the war with her husband Hermann Rothbart. An Austrian Jew, Hermann had worked as a leading Cold War strategist at the Pentagon before he assumed a decorated post at the Hoover Institution at Stanford University, where he finished out his days publishing rabid anti-Communist screeds. Politics aside, Hermann loved his *Wienerschnitzel*—it was a taste we shared in common from my earliest years—and no one in the world knew how to make a better *Wienerschnitzel* than Aunt Josey. Well, on the day in question everything was going along fine until I swallowed one of Aunt Josey's thin, delicious, amber-colored *Schnitzels*.

Don't ask me how it happened, just know this: When I went into the bathroom later to expunge that beautiful *Schnitzel*, I was sitting on the toilet, pushing and squeezing with rigorous effort when all of a sudden an elastic purplish thing that was my asshole sprang out of me. It's next to impossible to explain so just try to think of it like a metamorphosed belly button: My asshole went from being an innee to being an outee. In any case that evening I found my butt in my palm, it was staring up at me dark and primordial and when I screamed Aunt Josey rushed in. Her expression hovering between disgust and disbelief, she knelt down and pulled me across her knees, gathered my anus in her hand and pressed, first with her fingers and then with her thumb until she succeeded in squeezing my entire rectum back inside me.

That was just the beginning of my gut's rebellion. At seven I felt a sharp burn pulsing through my chest. It was like a fireball, day after day, meal after meal. By nine I was addicted to Tums. By ten I was shitting sloppy. The pain grew worse as I got older and ate larger meals at a faster speed, and by the time I left college I was primed for my first ulcer. I didn't see a doctor about it until the day when I knew I had to stop the burning. I was twenty three, living in a small city in Bolivia where I had been hired to write newspaper reports about a revolution that was just getting underway, so there was plenty to have indigestion about and one afternoon when the bullets stopped flying and the tear gas died down, I walked into a clinic.

Indians were shuffling around in tire sandals spitting coca leaves on the floor of the ward as I sat there awaiting my appointment. I had asked to see a foreign doctor and finally a German gastroenterologist came out to greet me (don't ask me why a Jew is confronted with German doctors and German diagnoses everywhere he goes). The man was thick in the jowls and neck and he reminded me of Captain Kurtz because as he led me to the surgery table he recounted how he had come to South America to complete his residency training and wound up three decades later still stranded in the Bolivian wilderness. A nurse slathered cold gel inside my mouth and switched on the laughing gas (I told Kurtz I had already tasted enough gas in the street fights with the army but he ordered her to turn it on anyway). She gave me an open plastic mouthpiece to bite on as Kurtz inserted into it a rubber tube affixed with a bug-eye camera. Kurtz was shimmying the tube like a chimney sweep down my throat as I watched the proceedings on a black and white television set, coughing and choking as he pushed the camera deeper through the buttery pink folds and chambers of my esophagus. Attached to the tube was a tiny sharp pair of tweezers and each time Kurtz pushed a button, the tweezers plucked a bit of skin off the wall of my gut. The plucks left a trail of bleeding spots behind them and when the tube reached the upper lining of my stomach, he saw it: the dark red splotch.

I coughed up a bucket of saliva and after the laughing gas wore off Kurtz said, "Your svincter muscle is veak. It does not block the acid vich shoots up from your stomach and the acidic juice has burned a hole."

"A hole?"

"Loss of tissue… inflammatory… disintegration…. Let us hope it is not Barrett's vich could be cancerous," he said.

"Jesus doctor, I'm only twenty three."

"Ja."

"Is it possible to be this ill this young?"

"Ja." After a pause he said, "Tell me, do you eat large quantities of food?"

"Yes."

"Do you eat very quickly?"

"Yes."

"Stop doing both and take these pills."

Kurtz handed me a packet of seven purple capsules. I eyed the capsules with the desperate hope of a dying man who believes his cure is within reach. I recalled the image of my grandfather Abram with the small silver tin that he kept at all times in his breast pocket. He would shake tiny white tablets from the tin which he chewed and digested with every meal, biting into them loudly and releasing belches in between.

"How long will I need to take these?" I asked.

"Possibly forever," Kurtz said. Then with benevolent hands he escorted me to the sliding glass doors that opened, showering me in sunlight as I stepped back out into the acrid air of a Bolivian war zone.

* * *

It was early March and I was rummaging through Eduardo's kitchen one morning, looking for something to put in my belly, when the phone rang and Frau Löscher's smoke-battered voice came on the other end.

"Ach, *guten Morgen*, Herr Krumm, how good I reached you. We haven't spoken for ages!"

"Frau Löscher," I said, bracing for what was coming next. "I'm sorry I didn't call the studio. I've been sick for some time."

"Ach, no bother, no bother," she croaked, and I missed her next joke in German. After a silence she went on, "We'll be discussing the Middle East on Friday, Herr Krumm. Tunnels from Gaza, Iran's support of Hezbollah, talks with Palestinian leadership. We want to especially focus on Washington's overtures to Syria. Will you be available to join us?"

Now there's something you have to understand. I had promised myself, after a particularly humiliating episode the previous autumn in which I'd got stuck defending America's drug war in Colombia, that I would stop going on television

66

to discuss global issues I knew little about. With millions of viewers watching and a German network's reputation at stake, any other approach seemed unsafe, unwise and unethical. Though you could also say those same terms defined my profession.

Different people use different names for the job I do. I usually tell people I'm a Media Auxiliary and leave it at that. In theory I spend my days researching and reporting and writing the news though in truth my hours are spent hovering online waiting for the news to reach me. I live in an over-stimulated age and I therefore require over-stimulation; barring illness, sex or travel, I am never not waiting for the news because the screen has made an addict of me. I have willingly handed over months and years—you might call them *the best years*—of my life to the screen, chained to it, locked there in a helpless state of waiting for news the way a man on dialysis is affixed to numerous tubes that are relentlessly pumping fresh blood into his veins. After all, what's fresh is what matters: what's new, what's instant, what hasn't already been chewed up and spit out by other Media Auxiliaries like myself. We're in a mad race together, the MAs and me, feeding off and devouring one another as we split and drain and waste our hours absorbed in a world that isn't visible, accurate, candid or even real: It is online. Online is my business. I digest shadows on the screen until the news pops up. Then I digest the news and reprocess it so other MAs can digest and reprocess what I have served them. I work quickly—oh yes, you've got to be quick in this trade because everyone's got bloody words to sell and they sell them cheap. I sell them cheap. Even when there's nothing to do and nothing to say a Media Auxiliary has to be saying something. As Evelyn Waugh once wrote: "News is what a chap who doesn't care much about anything wants to read… And it's only news until he reads it. After that it's dead."

I'll tell you, there was a time when I liked my job and when I even considered myself lucky to be doing what I do. But those days have passed. Stealing words, fomenting words, selling words has become an agony to me which is why I have supplanted my underpaid duties as an MA with my overpaid appearances on TV. Sitting in a stiff blue armchair with the glare of studio lights in my retina, now that's a pleasure! Who doesn't like a freshly ironed suit massaging his shoulders and a free breakfast of buttered pretzels with sweetened coffee churning in his gut? Perhaps the best part of going to the studio on Fridays is the odorous caked-on powder that Jana, the makeup artist, employs to discolor my face. Jana has big blue eyes and large perfumed breasts that she keeps thrust under my nose for minutes on end as she dabs peach toner on my cheeks and chin and forehead to keep the shine off. When the cameras are rolling I'm still feeling dizzy from the coconut palm essence I've been inhaling off Jana's chest, but I'm a professional and even through intoxication I'm able to perform. I've prepared my lines and rehearsed my role and as I sit on the bright-lit crescent stage with three commentator cranks bludgeoning me with attacks (I'm the American, I give the "view from Washington" so naturally I get bludgeoned), my defense hinges on an arsenal of tricks. I can disapprove with a headshake, deflect with a cocked brow, doubt with a squint. I may be dying in the trenches of auxiliary exchange (bantering without authority is the lowest form of banter) but I know when to interrupt with an important-looking finger and when to parody a laugh. When I'm on screen I have the smile of a jackal and enough qualified facial ticks to join a circus. It's true I have no business speaking to millions of viewers on air. My thoughts are meandering, my opinions libelous, my participation tiresome. Yet it's what I'm paid to do: to sit down in the living rooms of people already paralyzed by the prospects of nuclear war and terrorism and climate change and to threaten them with those scenarios further.

It's not that I am dishonest in my job, mind you, I'm not out to con anyone. I splash in the truth here and there. Between parentheses. Behind commas. In advance of questions. But the fact is I gave up long ago trying to convince people that I think and speak for myself. Perhaps this is, after all, my greatest asset and it's why Frau Löscher and the TV station keep calling me back: because I'm expert at taking other people's ideas, proposals and positions and passing them off as my own. In the end, I've learned, conviction is what counts. It doesn't matter what you say—if it is true or false, if you believe it or if you don't—what matters is how you say it. My job is simple because it's always the same. If we're talking about Iraq or Pakistan, the Balkans, Chavez, Ahmadinejad or Sudan: Whatever the crisis or debate, I argue it from Washington's eyes. I am the pilloried man. I take it on all sides and I take pride in being pilloried. I've received dozens of hate letters. They call me everything; one even said, "If you're going to have a Jew on the show, he should be an intelligent Jew!" Yet to this day I have not once turned down Frau Löscher's invitation to appear on screen. Maybe it is simply my need, as a disposable man with disposable intentions, to be noticed. I sold out in order to be heard and seen. I chose a pinch of glamour—and what a pinch, Frau Löscher!—over the pursuit of talent or satisfaction or real art. Becoming a news clown wasn't what I intended. But I had to do something. Even a disposable man must do something.

I took a moment to reconsider the offer as Frau Löscher's gravelly breath filled the receiver. I hadn't lifted a finger at work all winter. I needed the money.

"Danke, Frau Löscher," I said, keeping to the formal German script, "I'd be glad to."

"Ach, *wunderbar*! On Friday, then, at the usual time, Herr Krumm."

69

"At the usual time, Frau Löscher."

I stood up from the kitchen table and looked out at the fresh coat of snow blanketing the apartments on the Allee. The city looked radiant, shining with a clean white glow, and with a renewed sense of hope I put on a pot of tea, dusted off the computer screen and began to prepare for Friday's show.

NINE

EVGENY'S HANDS

Omsk, Siberia, 1941

Evgeny Antonovich Grunefeld curled his fingers around the small tin cup which held his tea. That's what the men called it anyway, though they knew it wasn't that. The drink had a brown cloudy texture and a lacquer taste, like water mixed with vinegar and earth, so to remind themselves that they were men and not animals they called it tea. The tea warmed the cup that Evgeny clutched first in his right hand, then in his left, passing it back and forth as it was too small for both hands with those long corded fingers to hold at once. He could recall only months ago when the fingers were taut, sinewy irons, each one a delicate hammer, refined and unblemished with a raging animus as they struck the piano's ivory keys. But now Evgeny looked down at appendages he did not recognize as his own: pale, stiff and functionless, no more than knuckle and bone. Now they were fingers that could not feel, much less glide through Chopin's Sonata No. 2 in B-flat minor, but at least, he thought, they could hold his cup of tea, or anyway what the men called tea.

Evgeny Antonovich joined the men at Omsk Workers Camp following the bright summer afternoon when he clutched his side and the guards carried him screaming off the train. Josey was hanging on to him crying, "Bubi, no! Bubi, no!" as the agony tore his stomach and passengers were pushed aside to let the soldiers take him. When he awoke he found himself lying on a wooden board in a dark hospital and there were nurses who came to see him. After the rip in his flesh healed into a nice purple scar, he was put to work in the brickyard alongside the other men. "Appendix is the least you'll lose here, little songbird!" laughed the chief guard and Evgeny stared at him in silence for he didn't understand the meaning.

What Evgeny understood was simpler: From darkness to darkness the men worked in the lonely yard out on the frigid plain mixing sand and laying mortar and carrying rocks and bricks. Guards stood by with rifles and pistols. They never told the men what the walled enclosure they were building would be for, they only watched them build it. "Perhaps after we finish the first wall," joked a worker named Oleg, "and the second and the third and the fourth, we'll have a fortress suitable for our tomb." The other men laughed. It was a special skill Oleg and the men had. They knew when to laugh and they knew when not to laugh but Evgeny knew neither the one nor the other and he especially didn't know it on the cold November night when his fingers curled helplessly around the tea. What happened was this:

The men had returned from the brickyard amid speculation that the temperature was already minus twenty. Some said ten, others fifteen, but the speculators said twenty. Their arguments and posturings against the cold, and against each other, were enough to make the night pass more quickly; the discussion alone made them feel that little bit warmer. The men told stories and shared memories as they recalled the joys of springtime. Evgeny was squatting beside the cauldron with its simmering bed of coals as the men hovered around the barrack chattering restlessly to keep warm. Some stood hard as stones, willing off the cold. Others rocked back and forth, shifting their weight from foot to foot in an effort to simulate movement and generate even the slightest heat. They wore scarves bound tightly around their necks and faces leaving only a gap where their eyes shined through. The luckier ones had caps with fur flaps over the ears and most men enjoyed the further insulation of a thick beard. Only Evgeny's boyish, oblong twenty one-year-old face, punctuated with two dark narrow eyes and a nose that ran in a sharp curve right off the end, was clean-shaven and bared to the cold. His face reflected a pale bluish light from the flames that licked around the base of the cauldron as he sat, absent from the men's talk, absorbed in a world of his own where the melody had gone silent.

Scenes from his childhood darted past, beginning with the day Papa first set him on the round wooden piano stool and his hands groped across the cold white keys and oh! the magic, how alive the instant dialogue that flowed through his fingers to create *sound*. At three Evgeny was playing beautifully, at six he wrote concertos and by ten he was turning Beethoven sonatas into jazz and oh! the people clapped, they clapped when he played, they clapped when the melodies rushed through him and Papa was proud, yes, proud of his little Bubi who at twelve played on the radio shows and at fourteen was brought to the Café Metropolis, Kovno's premier club on Laisves Aleja, where he entertained under the dim smoke-filled lights the ladies in their fashionable hats and skirts and the moustachioed men in suits who came to hear him. Evgeny still remembered the feeling as hundreds of eyes fixed on him and waiters hurried drinks and cakes under the chandeliers while Rachmaninov etudes and Schubert waltzes and concertos by Brahms poured from him like water from a glass that was continually overflowing.

Evgeny remembered other scenes, too, like the time Papa sent him to receive help at the special school—"the best money can buy," he said—and also to the doctors who used a language he didn't understand, words like *personality this* and *schism that* and *split phrenia something or other*. Evgeny even remembered the day when Josey held his hand and they rode the train to Zurich where the hospital was white and cold and the doctors put the electricity inside him and oh! it burned oh! it hurt, then Evgeny didn't remember a thing but when it was over Josey gave him a bar of chocolate on the train ride home and asked him, "Bubi, now what would you like to do?" and Bubi looked out the window at the cows in the green fields and said, "Now Josey sweetest, I want to take a trip around the world!"

If Evgeny had known when to laugh and when not to, perhaps he would chuckle at the cruel joke now that he had gotten what he asked for: a trip around the world all the way to its most extreme and unbeloved point. But just then, after studying the gnarled strips of flesh that were curled around his tea, Evgeny's ears perked up because Oleg was telling the men a story. Evgeny liked Oleg. He was one of the kind men. He was short and strong and he helped Evgeny hauling the bricks in the yard. Now he was telling the men about a girl from his school days named Mashka. "She was a big-bottomed girl and a whore to the bone and after class we would lure her to the forest," said Oleg, "because Mashka was famous, Mashka would do anything, she would insult you and kick you until you had her against a tree with her pants around her ankles and you were wriggling up inside her." (Evgeny looked at Oleg who made a dance like he was wriggling up inside her, and this caused the men to laugh.) "Well there was a game we used to play where one of us would pin Mashka against a tree trunk and while she was pinned there, squirming with her knickers on the ground and her legs up high, we asked her if there was any man on earth who she wouldn't let wriggle up inside her. 'Charlie Chaplain?'" Oleg said as he mimicked a schoolboy humping Mashka against a tree. "'Sure!'" he imitated Mashka in falsetto voice, which got the men laughing further. "'Henry Ford?' 'Why not!'" The men laughed some more. "'And Stalin? Would you let Our

Father Stalin wriggle himself inside you?' Then Mashka with a cock deep in her would get flaming red and shout, 'Stalin! Are you crazy? I wouldn't fuck Stalin in a million years!'"

The barrack fell instantly silent. Not a hush from the men, though they beamed at one another with laughing eyes. All was still but for those two quick, unaccounted for bursts of laughter which erupted just then from Evgeny's throat. "Haha! … Haha!" Two laughs, sharp and ecstatic, which echoed through the barrack as clear as the name that preceded them. The men's eyes darkened. They stood there staring at Evgeny, pitying the child so ignorant of his crime. The question on all the prisoners' minds—*Had anyone heard him?*—was answered momentarily by the sound of a guard's aluminium flask being opened outside the barrack. Nothing to be done. The men hurriedly resumed conversation, speaking in dull tones, trying to pass the time before their dinner soup was served.

Later that night, as the men tossed uneasily on their wooden bunks, two guards entered the barrack and picked up Evgeny from his bed. They walked him silently out the flap entrance and into the frigid night. Then they placed him in a cell without air or light so he had no idea if the day had arrived or if it had already passed. Evgeny shivered in the blackness, hands clutched together. His fingertips found a home in the loose spaces of flesh where the sound once moved. His wrists were twigs. The blood stopped moving through his arms. When they unlocked the cell two days later what they found was a shrivelled body, frozen and dry and curled up like a sleeping baby with its hands still folded. Two prisoners were ordered to bury the body in the forest beyond the barrack. They rolled Evgeny out there in a wheelbarrow. Then they took turns with a shovel and dug the hole. It was a small hole, for after stripping off his shoes, coat and pants, Evgeny looked as thin and weightless as a piece of wood.

When the men finally raised up the barrow, it wasn't but a feathery corpse that slipped out of it. "We could have covered him in soil six inches deep," one of them said when they returned to the barrack, and there was no more speculation that evening about the cold nor any jokes that the men felt like telling.

TEN

PRENZLAUER BERG MAN

After my spotty TV performance about Hezbollah and the headache in Israel, I rang up the Kaiser and nailed him down for an evening *Schnitzel*. Then I went out like most Prenzlauer Bergers go out on Saturdays, whether they want to or not, and strolled through the weekend crowd at Kollwitzplatz. The market was in full swing. Wörtherstrasse stood cluttered in stalls, kitchens, vans and canopies as the men and women of the Berg with their BMW-sized baby strollers elbowed through. Kollwitzplatz wasn't where I wanted to be. It bored me. It outpriced me. The atmosphere of plenty—of glib spending, sated consumption and matter-of-fact ease—depressed me. Who did these Bergers think they were flashing healthy blasé smiles as they tunneled through mountains of artisan breads and exquisite cheeses and an overflow of organic produce that no African village could afford? Dressed in felt-stitched hats and hand-carved clogs, the Bergerati went about their Saturday gorging effortlessly on *Currywurst*, Baltic bass, deluxe vegetable crèmes and nuts embalmed in sweetener. I wanted none of it and yet, to my astonishment, I once more found myself circling Kollwitzplatz like a planet hugged by gravity circles the sun. Unable to snap my orbit, I lagged and hovered around the periphery of the square because there was something about it which I found supremely attractive and also mesmerizingly dull. Sedate, picturesque, unbearably middle-class: that was Kollwitz. It was Prenzlauer Berg. My Berg. My Berlin.

They say Napoleon's architect rebuilt the Berg in accordance with a single law: that no building should rise taller than the width of its street. This created a marvelous effect: The Berg may belong to Berlin but its heart is in Paris. In the decades before I got here the district was a gray drab place inhabited by sulking workers of the GDR. Now reincarnated, the Berg feels like some elite island nation floating atop Europe. Its smooth cobblestone streets are as wide and cozy as canals, allowing swathes of sunlight to reach the buildings' bottom floors. There is no better place to walk than the Berg which is why I would walk there for hours at a time, aiming and arriving no place as I glided under the linden trees and gazed up at the handsome neo-baroque, neo-renaissance, neo-classical, neo-neo buildings in their pastel shades of salmon pink and lime green and piss yellow which all made me feel so deliciously at home. Berlin is a poor city—"poor but sexy," the gay mayor at the time called it—so naturally the sidewalks in the Berg are breaking to bits. They are crumbling, decaying, missing stones and detaching from one another as the ground grows wave-like from the giant roots of trees pushing up beneath them. But in the Berg, who's looking down? In Prenzlauer Berg everyone looks up! It is perhaps the only neighborhood in Germany where people exhale optimism and where the professed desire for less is actually a suppressed desire for *everything*.

Yes, somehow this Berg, the tidy epicenter of that fashionable Germanism known as *Lebenskunst*—the art of living— had become my home. But I was never exactly home there. Something about the place always felt out of reach and out of touch because in the Berg I got the eerie sense that I wasn't living in Berlin at all but in a post-Berlin: a Berlin that after growing stale and rotted and dying a not-so-natural death by not-so-natural causes had, like a cabaret zombie, sprung jubilantly back to life. After the Cold War a frenzy of capital resuscitated the Berg and this solitary, paranoid and remote neighborhood in the East became something that was not a lot like Berlin. Now it is crawling with wine bars and furniture boutiques and real estate firms selling off entire city blocks and putting whole streets up for sale. Now the people here are flocking to restorative sleep workshops and studying soul retrieval with the latest shaman who just stepped off the plane from Bangalore. They are receiving outlandish dental treatments and sending their children to pedicures.

It's no surprise the whole world wants to move here—everyone craves a piece of the buttery Berg. But what a loaf it is. Politicians and cultural enthusiasts say a new generation of luminaries will come from the Berg but I think it'll be just a lot of half-males. I think sloth will emerge from here. The fashions of the day have helped to produce a sleepy narcissistic laze in the Berg where everybody is beautiful and nobody looks at anybody any longer because they're too busy being looked at. They're too busy buying and wrapping themselves in Berg designer apparel, special handmade tailored-just-for-you designer goods fashioned from designer shops where you can get everything from designer watches and designer bags to designer shirts, socks, sex toys and designer cigars. They have it all in the Berg from designer candles made of designer wax to designer vases and lamps powered by designer bulbs. If you want designer frames or chandeliers or designer umbrellas they're here, so are designer belts and purses, napkin dispensers, pins and postcards. You can even find warm fuzzy designer underwear, designer pillows and satin ties and robes and caps and designer vinaigrette bottles, and if you want to commit yourself to the antiquated art of letter writing you can purchase the Berg's designer stationery and mail it in designer envelopes using designer stamps. That's right, the commerce is plump and it's feminine in the Berg, and really a lean male here doesn't stand a chance which is why it is in the Berg, and precisely here, where the disposable man thrives best.

I don't think the Kaiser would fault me for saying it and I hope you understand what I mean when I tell you that the disposable man is, in fact, the Prenzlauer Berg man. He is your modern man who has shaken the burden of masculinity off his shoulders and now stands gleaming with a well-oiled glass-eyed look of boredom. The Prenzlauer Berg man has thrown away his sword and all the edges it implied. He lives with comfort and predictability now; he lives the life that is handed to him rather than the one he formerly imagined he might seize. Dressing like a child he sports low-cut sneakers and loud t-shirts; it's an expensive style but he makes it look cheap and he hides behind a suave clipped beard if he is able to grow one. The Prenzlauer Berg man likes women—oh yes, he spends his days dangling and his nights drinking in search of the next stiff lay—yet finds himself sadly indistinguishable from the cadre of gay men who surround him. Not only does he look like them but he talks and acts likes them. The Prenzlauer Berg man is like a dog who has emerged from the operating room with only a vague notion that his testicles have gone missing. There is no sense of urgency or conflict written on his face because the Prenzlauer Berg man is never in a rush—there isn't after all any place he has to be. So he spends his hours sipping from foaming cups of coffee or foaming glasses of beer. He is never without foam around the lips. The foam is in his nature. He drinks it because it reminds him of himself.

Now you can go back to what the writer Leonard Kriegel once remarked, that "manhood, once a prize to be wrested from life, is now viewed as an embarrassment, an encumbrance to living successfully," and herein lies the dictum of the Prenzlauer Berg man. Ask where the real male inside him went and the Prenzlauer Berg man will stare at you with a hurt look. He is offended and shocked because he knows no other type of man than the one he has become; the real male, it must be said, went out of fashion too long ago for him to remember so he stopped trying. The change he underwent wasn't exactly his fault, he simply got caught up in the "androgynous drift" and he let the tide carry him. He stopped worrying about what his nature *is* and began listening instead to those who told him what it *should be*. In a sense the Prenzlauer Berg man was the smart man: He recognized there was a new breed of males to contend with, so he joined the breed. It isn't that he desired to be neutralized and fixed yet that is what has happened. Now the Prenzlauer Berg man is just surviving. He recalls a time when there was hunger in his gut but he has forgotten what the hunger feels like. He knows he is tired and yet he can't be certain most mornings that he has even woken up. That is why when the Prenzlauer Berg man speaks he is almost silent. Words drip out of him softly and slowly like water from a bum faucet. His voice is a voice normally reserved for concert halls and university libraries because the Prenzlauer Berg man isn't only afraid of being heard—he is afraid he might hear himself! The Prenzlauer Berg man knows he is living in an age when masculinity is suspect and the ideas of men are suspect, too, so he flashes a cream-filled smile at the world and who can blame him? The Prenzlauer Berg man has eaten at the table, enjoyed his fill, and is now being handed the check.

* * *

I pressed the buzzer outside the Kaiser's apartment on Kastanienallee and took out my pouch to roll one. I called Bruno the Kaiser because he had a reluctant king's aura about him. He was a mock Kaiser: a Kaeser who should have been a Kaiser. Bruno came from a family that once made cheese on the Rhine. They were filthy cheesemakers and their name was Käser and when they got to America it became Kaeser.

Bruno told me about his grandfather who used to put him to sleep with stories of a rowdy foul-smelling cheese named Schmierkäse. Schmierkäse got into all kinds of adventures. He was loathed but also envied for his potency. He smelled so bad it earned him respect. Every family has its heroic myth. That was Bruno Kaeser's.

Bruno lived on the top floor on Kastanien and he had it good: tall ceilings, pine floorboards and a giant pair of windows that looked west across the canyon of baroque buildings on Oderbergerstrasse toward the trees at Mauerpark. It was a cock's perch and it should have made Bruno feel every bit the Kaiser that he was. He even had his lovely Spanish girl Rosa up there living with him—Rosa with her ripe hips, dark hair, buoyant chest and gray leopardine eyes; Rosa who made him beef *guisado* and luscious Valencian rice and it didn't bother Bruno that they had little to discuss because Rosa smothered him in kisses and cute words and the tinny maternal sounds of love. But all of that wasn't enough for the Kaiser whose preoccupations ran deep.

"Be right down," his voice crackled through the intercom. Right down for the Kaiser meant right after he finished his beer, rinsed his dish, checked his email one last time, kissed Rosa goodnight, then filled his water bottle—adding lemon, always with a spritz of lemon—before bounding down the five flights of stairs. The Kaiser was constantly thirsty and he was constantly in a hurry and no doubt the two were related. He was dying of thirst. He thought it was a condition. I thought it was so he could drink water and keep his mouth busy when he wasn't talking. The Kaiser took water everywhere he went and he talked everywhere he went. He talked so much he managed to talk himself right out of his first marriage to a good Midwesterner named Ursula. "Hey baby if anything changes I'll let you know, otherwise assume I love you," is what he told her. Bruno and Ursula were living in

New York at the time, he was jobless and she wasn't getting pregnant and one day she stopped assuming. After dinner one evening she told him she'd been accepted to graduate school in Michigan.

"In what?" he asked, innocently enough for a guy who hadn't learned to listen.

"Pharmacology." He shrugged as his wife put her bowl in the sink and left the kitchen. A month later Bruno was on a plane to Prague. He told Ursula he would return, just needed to shake things up a bit and redefine his "purpose." He spent six months there working at a bookstore called Shakespeare and Sons, and when the Czech scene didn't do it for him any longer he hopped north to Berlin. Soon he met Rosa and started in writing his colossal text, and Ursula and Michigan became a distant memory. For years the Kaiser worked on that colossal text, feverishly and obsessively struggling to complete what he called his "treatise on modern malehood." It wasn't that he hoped to achieve anything with the treatise. Bruno didn't believe in achievement or ambition or accomplishment or any of it. As he put it: "I don't climb ladders because there isn't any place I want to reach."

I watched the good-looking women strutting past on Kastanienallee and was just about to throw down my cigarette when the heavy wooden door swung open. The Kaiser stepped out and his first words set the tone. "It's killing me, Max, it's killing me."

He had on a brown leather bomber and a gray fedora with the brim turned up. Beneath it burned two dark mercurial eyes shaped like olives. Bruno was dark and hairy all over; he liked to joke that he was descended from a lost tribe of Mongols. Thirty five, well-built, with biceps like eggplants and a chest inflated for battle, Bruno should have been a specimen of strength and model of vitality. Instead you could already see the old man creeping into him. He had a weary look, tired, like he had seen too much of the world too fast and expected nothing new. Bruno considered himself the punctual type, he never showed up very early or very late, yet when he arrived something in his eyes told you he was already leaving, or perhaps that he had already left. He was like an animal that has devoured the flesh of life and for whom only the carcass remains.

"What are you looking at, another six months?" I asked as we set off around the corner toward Schönhauser Allee.

"Six, ten, a year, fuck if I know, I can't finish the goddamn thing. The middle is weak, it doesn't have an ending and I don't like how it starts. You remember how it starts?"

"I do and I don't think it's weak at all," I said, trying to keep the Kaiser's ship from sinking in the first five minutes. "You're making progress, I know it."

Ironic it was me doing the sympathizing. After all, hadn't Bruno just skipped south to Spain with Rosa for the winter, leaving me up here in cuckolded solitude to bleed out my curse? At the Kulturbrauerei we hung a right and took Knackstrasse toward Kollwitzplatz.

"It's the spark, Max. I'm not feeling the spark. Lost the hunger, or something." The Kaiser pulled out his pouch, dug in his front pocket for a paper and started to roll one.

"You didn't lose it. It's like everything, Bruno, you just have to stay—"

"You know this whole thing, the whole goddamn treatise and what I'm trying to say, Max, boils down to four things: Strength. Courage. Purpose. Necessity. That's it! Those are the four elements, like air, earth, water and fire. That's what we've lost: Those four qualities are what used to define men from women and now they are what define women from men. But this damn text, I'm just not—"

"You'll finish it," I said, sensing a critical moment to interrupt him. "Just keep—"

"But it's eating me alive!" he shouted. At the corner of Kollwitzplatz he lit his cigarette. The Kaiser's eyes were black, immense, searching desperately in the flame for some kind of answer.

"Why not write it as fiction?" I asked as we passed Bill Clinton's old haunt, the Gugelhof, before veering east toward the Wasserturm.

"Everyone's writing fiction."

"You're still young, you can make the switch."

"It's not about age, Max, shit, everyone's a young author these days. You can be fifty and still be a young author. As long as you're not dead you're a young author. No, fiction's not the form for what I'm saying, what I'm trying to say..."

As his voice trailed off I remembered a conversation I once had with a Greek philosopher-peasant on the island of Amorgos. The peasant told me: "A man's happiness in life depends on three things: He must accept the world as it is, he must accept himself for who he is, and he must discover his office in life. If he does those three things, he will be a happy man."
As I looked at the Kaiser, now staring down woefully at the cobblestones while feverishly inhaling his tobacco, I saw a man who was anything but happy. More frankly he was tearing himself to bits. The Kaiser was consumed with time. You could see the clock ticking there inside him as he walked. He said he felt the constant loss of time around him and, as a result, had become a man who timed himself through life: measuring the seconds, monitoring the minutes, abdicating the hours. The Kaiser was never not at a loss over time and so he was never not elsewhere. *Goddamn time!* he would sometimes curse as if time itself, not what he chose to do with it, was his obstacle.

We passed Café Wronski where demure couples sat sipping from tall glasses of Riesling and poking their forks at mounds of *Strudel*. Poor Kaiser, I thought, apart from finishing his colossal text there wasn't anything in the world he sincerely wanted. It wasn't that he had failed, as he felt many in our generation had failed, to become a man. If anything the Kaiser had uber-male charisma. He exuded a violent charm that people absorbed like sponges, soaking him up, sniffing around that vital thing inside him like hyenas encircling a wounded lion. The Kaiser didn't keep many friends. It's possible, in fact, that aside from me he had none. He welcomed the solitude because he knew what he was searching for was a mightier, more rugged, more immortal experience of life than anyone could help him find. He kept his distance from the world with those dark paintbrush eyebrows which seemed to tremble as he gazed across the chasm separating his pupils from your own. The distance could yawn open like a fissure at any moment; you'd be talking to the Kaiser when suddenly a vacancy, like some flash flood, washed out his face. His deep black eyes would turn to glass and it was as though he had stopped hearing you, stopping seeing you, as his expression became impassable and he retreated into some hopelessly remote place that not you or anybody could see. That is when the Kaiser ignored you and ignored everything for the clock that was ticking so loudly inside him, and when he would finally draw the restless darks of his eyes away from yours, at the deepest point before their meeting, what you saw was a bonfire of gloom. His eyes seemed to say: We live in a solitary place called Elsewhere.

It was with relief that we arrived at Metzer Eck on the corner of Strassburgerstrasse and Metzerstrasse, and ascended the stone steps. The restaurant was warm with its familiar dim-lit charm. The walls had a rough mustard-colored texture and were strung with old black and white photographs and landscape paintings set in thick brown frames. Rustic iron chandeliers dangled from the ceiling and wicker shades lit the small tables in the back room. Finally seated, the Kaiser looked able to breathe again.

"Hear anything from Lotte?" he asked.

"No."

"No emails, nothing?"

"I saw a flyer for a show she's doing in Bielefeld."

"Bielefeld, shit."

"Yeah."

"She really dragged you through it."

"Yeah."

"Screwing that director from Mannheim and all."

"Düsseldorf."

"Right," he said, lifting his gaze, "Düsseldorf."

The middle-aged barmaid Helga approached, her stout chest covered in lacy frill. "*Was möchtet ihr?*"

"*Zwei grosse Bier, zwei Schnitzel, bitte,*" the Kaiser answered.

"Vith or vithout potatoes?"

"With," he said, and the moment she left he was back on his horse. "But what did I tell you, Max? First thing I said, 'Don't marry a German.' Then I said, 'Don't marry the granddaughter of an SS man.' Didn't I? I said keep your distance from the Nazis, isn't that what I said?"

"Probably."

"Not probably, that's *exactly* what I said. But who am I to talk? I fucking married into middle *middle* America which is pretty much the same thing. Marriage ain't a hundred yard dash, man, it's a marathon and we both fell at the first mile. But shit, it's all the same who you marry anyway, isn't it, I mean marriage is just the place men go once they've lost interest in being men."

"Not necessarily."

"Max, don't bullshit me. Losing interest is the single most important ingredient for a man to want to marry. He's had enough of the thing that makes him feel alive—adventure,

87

solitude, fear, exhilaration, hope, desire, sex—so he settles for the thing he knows he's *not* but goddamn it must be his. He's tired of life as he fears it so he marries and reduces himself further. He becomes a secondary feature to himself. That's right, he's a secondary man."

"Secondary," I said, weighing the Kaiser's meaning. Helga returned with two sweating mugs of Warsteiner and set them on the coasters in front of us.

"Sure he is," the Kaiser went on, looking enlivened now as he pulled out his pouch to roll one. "When a man puts on the warm gray coat of matrimony it makes him sweat and that's how he knows he's gotten with the program, see, but the program has another name, it's called Death and all of a sudden our secondary man wakes up to find it's the only program he's got left."

I nodded and started to roll one.

"So here's the married man who wants to vanish, right, because he just traded in the most valuable thing he's got—his freedom for fuck's sake—and all he got in return was the illusion of certainty and ease. But he won't be certain and he won't have ease, not in marriage, no way, because now he's gotten with the program, right, he's gambled away his independence and chosen safety over selfishness when selfishness was the only thing that ever made him happy. Isn't it the only thing that makes us happy, Max?"

"Could be. But we're also looking for something more than just ourselves, aren't we?"

"Yeah yeah of course, of course, and it's all going to end in disaster anyway whether you marry or you don't," he said, and just then I saw the gulf open in the Kaiser's eyes. Maybe he was contemplating death or maybe he was thinking about the way his own false yes had betrayed an honest no with his mid-dle *middle* America. The Kaiser lit his smoke and was squint-ing toward the barmaid, lost in thought, when I retrieved him.

"We never talked about it but I had a pretty hard time this winter, Bruno, you know, recovering from—"

"Yeah yeah I know, the cuckold bit," he said, pinching a few loose hairs of tobacco from the mouth end of his cigarette.

"I'm just saying, things still feel kind of fresh, like I don't—"

"Thing is, Max, we don't hold the cards!" he silenced me. "Now hang on a minute because I've been thinking an awful lot about this and you know, your woman, my woman, it doesn't matter which because there's a basic law we know as disposable men and it's this: Her plans come first, not yours. You have to get that in your head, Max, all of us next-males have to get it in our heads: It's her work that matters, her ambition that counts. Not yours. She's the go-getter, the hungry one. Look at any woman out there," he said, waving his hand to Helga for two more beers, "look at any woman and what does she want? She wants a career, she wants status and security and recognition, all of it. She wants respect, she wants influence, she wants a name. But you and me, we don't want those things. We gave up wanting those things. We're on the backside of history now, my man. Those dreams of becoming something—a doctor, a lawyer, an engineer, a professor or whatever—those days are past. But we're better for it, Max. We don't need them, those identities, because we don't identify with them any longer. We spent centuries—man we spent fucking millennia!—trying to find ourselves and our egos and our purpose in our work: in what we *do*. We're weak and diminished now, Max, we're disposable because all that intention and all that drive is gone. There's nothing we're working for, nothing we want. We lost it and women took it and now they own it, it's theirs, and what do we own? What are we now? We're an accessory. We're adornments. Appendages. We're a sideshow. We're like the salad with the meal.

Face it man, Ursula, Rosa, Lotte, any woman out there: They don't need us, they don't want us, and I don't want to be a fucking salad."

He took a final swallow from his mug to make way for the fresh Warsteiners that had arrived.

"But Rosa digs you, man, you know she loves you and anyway doesn't all this just give us more freedom—"

"More freedom? Of course we've got more freedom! Freedom for what? We're free to do whatever the fuck we please and that's the problem," he said, pausing to light another cigarette. "There's no pressure, see, no obligation or need to even be or do or think anything at all. We should all be happy like big fucking house cats is what we should be. Think about it, Max, what made a man back in the day? His ability to earn money. His skills in the professions. His bravery fighting wars. His power over women. Now I'm not talking medieval, no, I'm talking two generations ago but now all of that has been stripped from us and handed back with our balls on a platter. Now don't look at me cockeyed like that because I'm not blaming chicks. I'm not. If I were them I'd do the same thing: I'd shove it all right back in our balls. We have to see ourselves for what we are, Max, see, that's what I'm trying to get at with the damn script. There's this historic shift going on right under our eyes and right under our skins because women changed and they made us change with them, and now what are we? What kind of man are you, Max? What do you do that makes you *you*? You've got nothing to show and nothing to prove. You're just another schmo trying to do what? There's nothing out there for you, Max, nothing for any of us. No responsibilities. Nothing to become. Not even any plans to make. Are you really going to spend your life building a career because you think it will tell you who and what you are? I'd rather be poor and nowhere right here in Berlin. It's comfortable like that too, isn't it? We gave up the dream a long time ago of being men, with men's desires and men's appetites and men's pride. Now we're just existing. We're just waiting."

"Waiting for what?"

"Don't know. Our death as a species, I guess. Or some kind of reemergence."

Our *Schnitzels* arrived. They were soaked in grease and bathed in a pool of creamy herb butter. I spread the butter across the crackling steak and brown-fried potatoes as the Kaiser swigged the rest of the mug and picked up his knife and fork.

"Marrying Lotte was a mistake," I said. "I get that."

"Mistake!" The Kaiser coughed up the first bite of his *Schnitzel*, his eyes widening.

"It was a mess, I never should have done it."

"Damn right you never should have done it because marriage is weakness, Max. We both did it and now look at us," he said, stuffing a fork full of pork and potatoes in his mouth and chewing it around. "We're just sniffing around the men we once were. We're unaccounted for, with nothing of use and nothing of value. That's what makes us disposable. You came to Berlin looking for something. Shit, we all came to Berlin looking for something but it doesn't mean we found it, does it? We're just following a hunch, that's all. We're living a belated dream. We're the unhappy grandsons who put our grandfathers on our knees to tell us stories. We're castoffs. We talk to stones in the street. We think we can outwit time because we came to a place where time looks like it's standing still. But it isn't, is it? Instead we spend our days thinking about what is worse: to be disposable or be disposed *of*. Our shadows do our breathing for us. You're gray, Max. You're as gray as your next-male generation. That's what we are: disposable men in a gray disposable generation."

"Still it's better than the harness, wouldn't you say?"

"True, it ain't no harness. No one's asking you to do a goddamn thing. No boss or woman or parent or friend is waiting for you to move a bloody inch." The Kaiser belched as he pushed away the plate. He took a pull on his Warsteiner and unfolded the pouch to roll one. "You know why I left America, Max? Because America wasn't my place, not any longer. The propaganda was getting to me: the advertisers and promoters and entertainers, the athletes, the vote thieves and criminal sons of bitches who run the country. The clutter of the empire, man, it was surrounding me like a siege, the circus of America was strangling me; it's still strangling all those poor motherfuckers who stayed home and didn't leave. But we fled, Max, like refugees fleeing a rising tide except in our case it was the gray tide of a gray generation that we couldn't escape," he said, squinting as he lit his smoke, "now see, I'm a refugee, Max, a refugee from all things: from professions and dollars, from weekend sales and Hollywood sweetener. I'm a refugee from the noxious headlines of a democracy that became a dictatorship. I fled it, fled our proud wasted nation with its lazy unimportant mornings when a man wakes up feeling weak inside from a pain he can't articulate, a pain more like an emptiness that's beating in his chest. Remember what old Rushdie wrote: 'I've come to America to be devoured.' Well fuck, Max, I left America *not* to be devoured. I'm one of those bawling sons of America, part of a revolution of orphans that swelled across the sea, surging back up on to the Old Continent—the land of our grandfathers! We swam back, Max, back into the drowned chapters of history. We returned to ashes and roots, ashes and roots. Your ancestors, my ancestors, they fled west and when it came our turn we fled east. We followed the trail back."

"For what? What do you think we're hoping to find?"

The Kaiser gave a disappointed look, exhausted. "How about some shots—let's do us a couple Jägers to clean the palate, what do you say?" Waving at the barmaid he shouted, "*Zweimal Jägermeister bitte!*"

I glanced at the clock on the wall, nearing midnight. The Kaiser didn't want Rosa to wait up for him and he also didn't want her going to sleep alone. I could see the clock behind his eyes ticking, hurrying us toward the closure. "You know what it is," he said in a voice that was suddenly quieter, calmer, almost conspiratorial. "We're just muddling through till we get our break. That's it."

"Our break?"

"Shit, Max, don't you understand? That woman Lotte cost you your balls."

"Yeah."

"You need to get your balls back."

"Yeah."

"So how are you going to do it?"

"I don't know."

"I know what I'd do."

"What?"

"Leave."

"Leave?"

"Yeah, just get the fuck out of here. Go do something, find something else."

"Funny you say it. Wayne and the fellas had an idea to—"

"Just fucking go," he said, winking at Helga as she arrived with our Jägers. We took them off the tray and slammed them.

"We're talking about a bike trip to Poland and I'm thinking I'll continue east."

"Doesn't matter where, Max, just get the hell out of here. Move on, there's nothing for you here, nothing for any of us. We're just hanging on and getting older and avoiding decisions. Go do something. East, where east? You mean Russia?"

"Lithuania."

"Lithuania? What for?"

"You know what for, it's where my family was from. Before Berlin, they lived in Kovno. Then they moved back, my great grandfather and great aunt and uncle. They got deported to Siberia and it saved them from the Nazis but something else happened, Bruno, I don't know what it was because none of them spoke about it. Something lingered, something I think they were ashamed of and never told me. Maybe I'll find it in the archives."

"What do you think you're going to find?"

"I don't know but my aunt—"

"The Einstein one?"

"Yeah, the Einstein one. She never should have gone back to Kovno before the war. She was living with her sister and my grandfather in Prague, they were all studying there and when Hitler invaded Sudetenland they left. My grandparents went west but Josephine, she returned to Kovno because her father and brother—"

"That idiot savant uncle you told me about, the pianist?"

"Yeah, the pianist, but this is something else. Something about the postcard, or before the postcard. Josephine could have saved herself. She could have gone with Abram and Elsa but she didn't. Something between the sisters—happened."

"And you think you're going to find it out in some Baltic wartime police charts?"

"Archives, Lithuanian archives. I heard you can just show up and ask to see your family files."

"For fuck's sake," the Kaiser said, snubbing out his cigarette.

"It's what I want to do. How about you, you feel like joining for a trip?"

"You know I'm too wrapped up here with my goddamn text," he said, and at the mention of the word his eyes went blank. It was like the whole messed up engine of his life was contained in that four-letter word: both what the *text* said and what the *text* did not and could not ever say. Men would stumble on, the human race would continue to breathe and survive with or without the publication of the Kaiser's colossal text, but I hesitated to consider what the failure to complete the treatise would mean for his own existence. We finished our beers in silence, the Kaiser rolled another cigarette and so did I, then we set a handful of euros on the table and stepped out into the March night, drifting, like the smoke of conversation, in opposite directions.

Eleven

A Sister's Lament

Los Altos, California, 1998

Before I can finish telling you about the young Josephine I never knew, I must tell you a thing or two about the old Aunt Josey I did know—the misshapen diabetic woman with a throaty voice who smothered me in lime-scented Eau de Cologne and wine-red lipstick and delivered into my mouth those formidable *Wienerschnitzels* along with gelatinous fruit cakes and chewable Vitamin C's as though it were me who was preparing for Siberia and not she who was recovering from it. A visit to Aunt Josey's never ended without her slipping two small bars of soap into my pocket at the door, "just in case." Aunt Josey's house smelled something like a laboratory what with all the vitamins and colognes and unused oily soaps she kept scattered around. But the medicinal odor was also no surprise, I suppose, since her scholarly, once-brilliant husband Hermann had suffered a stroke which left him, at 82, drooling and shitting himself in a wheelchair. During Hermann's late years, Josey had hired a strapping Bavarian woman named Inés to work as his caretaker. Inés had lean golden arms, long muscular legs and a big head of electric blond curls. She'd fled from some remote village at eighteen, flown direct to California and when her visa ran out she found work as a bodybuilding instructor for lonely house-wives in Walnut Creek. After Hermann's stroke Aunt Josey started making some calls and was relieved when she landed on "such a strong and capable German-speaking woman," so she offered Inés free rent and top pay to care for "*mein Baby, mein Lämmchen*," as she referred to her stricken husband.

No sooner had Inés entered Aunt Josey's home than she made herself indispensable. Inés lifted Hermann into and out of his chair with ease. She bathed him. She changed him. She cooked for him. She even sang to him in an airy alpine hymnal voice that reminded Hermann of the Old Country and made part of his mouth twist up into a grimacing smile. It made Aunt Josey smile, too, but her smiling didn't last long because the plump salary she awarded Inés had put the glitter in her eye. First Inés bought a white Mustang convertible (I remember her smell, a mixture of seaweed shampoo and backcountry herbs when she left the house all sexed up for a drive.) Then she dated a string of black boyfriends who cadged what they could (Aunt Josey's credit card disappeared on the day Inés went to see Notorious B.I.G. in concert at the San Jose Arena). Finally it appeared that Inés had afflicted as much as she rescued Aunt Josey while tending to her groaning, dreadfully impaired and soon-to-be deceased husband, but by that time it was too late.

A sort of madness overtook my poor aunt in those years that she dedicated to keeping her "little lamb" alive. I watched her suffer as Hermann spat and baaed like a sheep. His growls filled the room and I could see the old bleeder wanted to smile; his eyes were sparkling like a baby's on that bloated immobile face while his body sat dwarfed beneath the blankets heaped on his wheelchair as senseless words oozed out of him. But Aunt Josey never gave up on Hermann. I remember the way she would rush from the table as fast as her little rotund body could carry her, fetch a pad and pencil from the desk in the kitchen, and place it between Hermann's quivering fingers. "*Schreib, mein Kind,*" she implored, "*Bitte, schreib!*" and Hermann could gaze up at me with that wretched twisted smile as he scratched out the letters "y o u a r e g r o w i n g" before choking on his saliva and coughing his apple sauce supper all over the dining table. "Oh my baby, my poor poor baby, *mein Kleiner!*" wailed Aunt Josey, cleaning Hermann's mouth with a hand towel as Inés looked on from the sofa with the shiny pages of a *Victoria's Secret* catalogue fluttering in her fingers. "Oh my dear little one, *mein Lämmchen, mein Kind,* my darling!" Aunt Josey cried, hopelessly repeating the words while deep down she must have known it was she who was putting him through this mess. Aunt Josey should have let Hermann die long ago. It would have been the sensible thing to do. But Josephine had already had love stripped from her too many times in life and damned if she was about to let another beloved creature escape her grasp.

Yet escape he did. After Hermann's death, Aunt Josey's diabetes worsened. I was a teenager by then and I remember visiting her when she already had a channel the size of a bicycle tire running up the length of her arm. That's where they changed the blood three times a week. Sometimes I would accompany her to dialysis but the time I'm thinking of was a day when Inés brought Aunt Josey home, wrapped up in a red silk shawl with black sunglasses and a black beret. Her face was swollen and colorless except for two bright red streaks of lipstick, and there were spots all over her skin. She was exhausted from the machines and when she told Inés to wheel her into the bedroom, I followed. There, in the darkness, I joined Aunt Josey as she lay with her face turned toward the shuttered blinds and said in her quiet gravelly voice, "*Mein Kind,* I wish I had been braver."

"Aunty, you were very brave."

"I didn't do much. Not as much as I could."

"What could you have done?" I asked.

"Many things, things I cannot tell you, my dear, things that are too painful for me even now to think about, oh-oh-oh! the things I did not do."

"But Aunty you saved your father and you—"

"It is not enough!" she said and turned in the bed to face me with flaring eyes. "Do not argue with me, Maxie. There are things you do not know but you will know them one day." Then Aunt Josey's voice went husky and faint and she drifted into a half sleep. She was mumbling, fighting something. A memory. An experience. It was muddy what she was saying and she was suffering terribly but she persisted, mixing German with English and excited Russian until the mad exchange abruptly ended. Lying there, Aunt Josey was breathing heavily when all of a sudden in a soft, almost inaudible voice, she gasped.

"The baby."

"What baby?" I leapt to her side, shivered by the word. The chill was still running through me as I stood up and leaned close over her face. "What baby, Aunt Josey? What baby?"

"The baby," she repeated in a weak whisper, then fell asleep.

* * *

I went into Aunt Josey's bedroom the next morning and found her motionless, lying in the darkness. She made an effort to look at me. Her eyes were like glass covered with a murky gray film. She smiled a painful smile because she knew she was trapped there, waiting, with the smell of death around her. I helped Aunt Josey out of bed and into the chair which I wheeled into the dining room, setting her in the place where Hermann used to sit. I brought her a cup of tea and some chocolate cake from the fridge. "I am not supposed to eat the cake but they change my blood so often, what does it matter!" she laughed. Inés came in and helped Aunt Josey into a purple chemise sweater. She wrapped her favorite silk scarf around her neck, the black one covered in red birds and yellow flowers. Finally Inés handed Aunt Josey her beret and sunglasses and once she had finished painting her lips we were off. I accelerated the old Mercedes slowly out of the driveway and on our way to get Chinese food Aunt Josey didn't say much. She didn't take off her scarf or her beret or her sunglasses even after the lemon chicken arrived, and as we ate I couldn't help looking at the dark deep channel they had carved into her forearm. It was swollen blue, almost black, where they inserted the tube three times a week to drain her blood. It was the tube and the filthy dark channel that kept Aunt Josey alive just a little while longer, long enough for her to finish telling me her story.

Aunt Josey liked going to see the ducks so after lunch we drove out to the Baylands. I wheeled her along the path as people jogged and phoned and carried on their noisy lives around us. When Aunt Josey saw the ducks her broken sentences started up, so I sat down on a bench beside her as we watched the emerald mallards drifting through the water. "I met Aleksandr Solzhenitsyn some years ago and he asked me, 'Where did you learn to speak Russian?' I told him, 'I finished Stalin's University,'" Aunt Josey chuckled. "He understood me perfectly. But *mein Kind*, I never expected it to end this way."

I looked at the bicycle tire in Aunt Josey's arm.

"If you saw how elegant we all were before the war, and how handsome was your grandfather, oh! Abram was a dashing man. I was so young but your grandfather was good to me in Prague, a real gentleman, he took care of me and then— oh! so many things happened, what happened before the war and what happened during the war, they are too much for your old aunty to tell you, too many terrible things—"

"What terrible things?"

"I will tell you, the time they took Bubi from me was terri-

100

ble," she said, releasing a tired breath. "We were on the train from Kovno, they had put us into cattle cars with thin slats for windows that let in only bits of air and light. It was hot, oh! how hot *mein Kind*, so terribly hot and there were at least fifty of us pushed into the car without seats or benches so we put our blankets on the wood floor and we slept. Soon the smell started, it was a terrible smell and finally we couldn't breathe so the men built a toilet and then they built a shower and between the men who talked and the men who bored the holes I learned one thing: Jews are not mechanics. There we were, Russians, Poles, Lithuanians and Jews: the Lithuanians hated the Poles, the Poles despised the Lithuanians, both were blood enemies of the Russians and everyone forgot about the Jews! It was lucky for us because Bubi, you see, he was a big boy then, twenty or twenty one, he was tall with a handsome smile but he was just like a child. Every day Bubi would ask if our train was returning to Kovno. 'No Bubi,' I told him, 'they are taking us someplace very far away. Papa is out here somewhere. We must find Papa, Bubi, that is what we must do. You must be strong so we can look for Papa.' Of course Bubi didn't understand my words, they made no sense to him and when we received only small rations of bread he said, 'Don't we get a little bit of hot chocolate, Josey?' 'My Bubi!' I said, 'We don't have hot chocolate here. We have something like tea but it isn't really tea,' and Bubi couldn't understand that either. Poor, poor Bubi with his absolute ear."

Aunt Josey quieted for some moments while she watched the ducks floating on the pond's surface. She continued, "And then it happened, one morning as we were crossing the Asian steppe, Bubi leaned over with a great pain stabbing his side. He hugged himself and moaned for hours and when they stopped the doors swung open and guards violently carried him away. 'My poor Bubi!' I cried, 'Don't take my Bubi, no don't take Bubi!' I was holding on to his hands with all my life but they tore him from me. The guards beat me back inside the train and I cried and cried, oh my poor Bubi I cried."

Aunt Josey's pale spotted face was motionless behind her large dark glasses.

"You never saw Bubi after that?"

"I never saw Bubi after that and I will tell you, Maxie, after they took my Bubi I lost all hope. I had no Elsa, no Papa, no Bubi, no little—" Aunt Josey caught herself, pausing suddenly as a pair of ducks flapped their wings and ascended from the water. "Then one morning the train stopped and sunlight flooded the wagon and the whistle blew for us to get off. We had arrived at Barnaoul, a collective farm where they gave us narrow wooden boards to sleep on and soup that consisted of a spoon placed on a puddle of animal fat. I told you I had never worked a day in my life before Yakutsk but it's not quite true because I worked in Barnaoul. I worked in the fields picking beets and cucumbers and I worked on the combine gathering grain. You had to be fast on the combine, oh yes you had to be fast because the grain was pouring out and it never stopped pouring and you had to change the full sacks for the empty ones without spilling any of the grain, all the time keeping an eye on your sacks because no one was honest, everyone cheated, your comrades stole from you when you weren't looking—they stole your grain and your beets and your cucumbers and they took credit for the work they had not done. The only Russians I ever knew were thieves and liars, Maxie, but I will tell you, the thing I wanted most in Barnaoul was to contact Papa so one day I stopped and asked a farmer for directions to the post office. 'Look what tiny little hands you have,' the farmer replied, 'Have you never gone to work?' 'Yes I worked, but what good do these tiny hands do me?' I told him. 'But you didn't go to work every day,' he said. 'Yes I did but can you please tell me where I must go to find out where my poor father is?' 'You pass a field of grain on your right, then you cut through a field of clover and when you come to a field of wheat—' 'Can't you tell me to go to the right or to the left? I have no idea if wheat looks different from grain!' I said. The farmer was speechless. 'Did you never go to work?' he said again. 'Yes but I went through streets and I went with the bus and I went with the train and I did not go by foot!' I told him." Aunt Josey gave a hoarse laugh and coughed for a time. Finally she continued.

"It was a long time before I heard from Papa. Every morning after breakfast I walked to the post office where they tacked a list of names on the wall. Those were the people for whom letters had arrived. My name never appeared. I was ready to give up. But one morning I decided to make a last attempt so I went to the office and greeted Brasha the post boy. 'Brasha, how are you?' I said. 'Never mind hello, Josephine, here is a kiss!' Brasha answered, and he leaned his cheek close to my lips. Ah, so Brasha has something for me, I thought. I kissed Brasha and pulled the letter from his chest pocket. It was from Papa, sent from the North Ural Work Camp in Svertlovsk. At last I knew that Papa was alive! And then, a few weeks later, they put me on a ship and sent me down the Lena River, all the way to Yakutsk."

PART II

TWELVE

THE POSTCARD ARRIVES

New York, 1941

The sun had never felt so hot against his skin, the light so sharp, the air so wet, nor was a horizon ever battered by so much concrete, glass and steel as the day Abram Mikhailovich arrived, with Elsa's arm clutching his, on the shore of America. Seven days prior they had boarded the freighter in Liverpool, one of the last wartime vessels carrying emigrants out of Europe. Among the ship's passengers were three hundred and twenty one children being taken to safe haven in Nova Scotia. Abram and Elsa knew the risk. Their ship was flanked by British naval boats that escorted them for five days and five dark, unlit nights through waters thick with German submarines. Then, on the sixth night, the lights came on. Men lit cigars and toasted with cognac as women danced with hoisted skirts in celebration. The war was now behind them, the bombs and the sirens, the smoke and bloody faces and starving children and the weeping wives and caskets: all of it was behind them. When their ship finally approached land that June morning it was like a dream for Abram, who rubbed the sweat from his eyes as he stood on deck gazing at castle-like towers glowing on the burnt horizon. He caught a vision of his future like an acrobat, suspended there between the buildings, connected by bridges, balancing himself on this barbed unearthly skyline that was to be his home: Manhattan!

"KRUM-KOT-KIN. What kinda name is that?" barked the man at the registry. The official had orange flames of hair and a seedy cracked complexion. Some breadcrumbs were stuck in the foliage of his moustache and a yellowish film coated his short uneven teeth. When he spoke his lips sent tiny white particles of spit arching onto Abram's face.

"It is a Russian name, sir."

"Yeah I can see you're Russian." The official sniffed, glowering at the papers. The man's frown made Abram anxious and suddenly the heat was melting his skin. He glanced back at the sea of dark eyes bobbing in line behind them as streams of sweat crawled down his forehead, neck and arms. His shirt was soaked, his underpants clammy. The acids gurgling in Abram's throat threatened to erupt so he coughed to mask his discomfort. They'd heard the stories of waiting, questioning, medical exams, more waiting, interrogating and, finally, rejection. Perhaps their papers, hastily arranged by a fixer in London, were not good either? Were they missing a stamp from some office or other? Abram stood in silence, paralyzed by the possibilities. They could be turned back to re-cross the Atlantic like the thousand Jews on the *MS St. Louis*, but no! It would be too much to bear, and wasn't she, after all, a Jew, the woman Lazarus whose immortal words Abram had put to memory: "*With conquering limbs astride from land to land / Here at our sea-washed, sunset gates shall stand... Mother of Exiles. From her beacon-hand / Glows world-wide welcome; her mild eyes command.*" Those words, engraved on the tall green statue in whose shadow he and Elsa now stood, meant surely the Jew was a more welcomed and pitied species on this continent, prayed Abram as the sweat continued to pour off him.

The orangish man meanwhile remained hunched over their documents and passports—two dark, worn-out booklets that contained all of Abram's and Elsa's past and nothing of their future—when suddenly a smile snuck from behind his moustache. The official looked up at Abram, then back down at the passport, and said finally, "Here's what we're gonna do, Mista Krumkotkin. We're gonna let you and your wife in. But you're in the United States of America now and I don't care where you come from, Russia, Czechoslovakia, Poland, doesn't matter to me one bit because we don't go running around this country with long names no one can pronounce, see? So I'll tell you what we're gonna do, we're gonna take out the Russian bit—what is it, Communist, you a Communist Mista Krumkotkin? Coz if you're a Commie we're gonna put you right back there on that boat and send you back where you come from."

"I am not a Communist," said Abram with a level stare.

"Good, that's good, so here's what we're gonna do, we're gonna take the last part, the whole 'kotkin' and we're gonna dump it like this, see? We're gonna make a niiiiice clean end on your name coz you won't be needing it no more." Abram watched, breathless, as the man licked the tip of his red pencil and drew a slow thick line through the last six letters of his surname in the passport, then did the same to Elsa's. "That way people in this country can say it and understand it and you won't get caught up in a whole lot of unnecessary controversy you understand? We'll throw you an extra 'm' on the end, how's that? Looks better if you ask me. From now on your name's just Krumm, got it? That's all people gonna call you. Alright, Mista and Missus Krumm, welcome to America, next in line please step forward!"

Abram stood motionless, too bewildered to move. He thought of his father, Mikhail Jakobovich Krumkotkin, and his father's father, Jakob Alexeyevich Krumkotkin, and all the generations of Krumkotkins that had led to this point of final disembarkation. An argument was out of the question; he wasn't about to jeopardize their arrival. Abram turned and looked once more at the thousand immigrant eyes, black and ponderous, hovering in the shadows of the Ellis Island terminal. Then he gathered his documents, took Elsa's hand

and exited into the light. Blinded by sunshine, they emerged through the iron gate. A porter's whistle brought a taxi to them and Abram handed several coins to the porter, but as soon as the taxi started, Abram heard shouts and turned to see the porter chasing after their vehicle with a knife. The man lunged at the cab, cut the luggage belt and their suitcases crashed to the street. "You didn't pay me enough!" he yelled. So Abram dug in his pocket, handed the porter the remaining coins he had exchanged for three shillings, and they set off with New York's special greeting kiss behind them.

The couple spent their first weeks in a hotel on West Forty Forth Street. Then they took an apartment on East Seventy Ninth off Central Park. Abram soon got a job with the City Planning Commission drawing maps of Brooklyn for twenty five dollars a week. He rode the subway downtown each morning and he rode the elevator to the eighteenth floor each day and he applied himself at the desk like so many millions in that great pulsating machine of which he was now a part—New York City. Less than two months after their arrival Elsa announced her pregnancy. By October they had moved off the island into a larger, cheaper apartment located out on the edge of Queens in a place called Rego Park where goats still roamed the streets and English was spoken only as a last resort. The neighborhood was thoroughly Russian, so Russian that if Abram squinted hard enough and waited for the smells and sounds to reach him, he could imagine himself strolling through the streets in his native land.

But this was not Russia. It was not Europe or anything he could recall from his previous life and with every passing month Abram felt the memories of home grow dimmer. Smolensk, Riga, Berlin, Prague—even London, where the Krumkotkins lived through the first two years of the war, where Abram's duty was to stand on the rooftop of their boarding house and spot enemy planes—none of it seemed present now. Elsa, after Prague, had suffered a breakdown and required psychoanalytic treatment, but even that trauma now felt remote. Abram still had not heard from his parents in Smolensk. Nor had Elsa heard from her father or her sister in Kovno. Abram worked at his job. Elsa's belly grew larger.

Then, on the next to last day of December in 1941, a chilling wind blew sheets of snow through the rutted streets of Queens and a tall, finely dressed man showed up at the Krumms' door. Introducing himself in German, the man greeted Abram with a firm handshake and an inquiring smile. He said his name was Valentin Bergmann, that he worked as an assistant for Dr. Professor Albert Einstein at Princeton University, and that he had been crossing New York City now for one week in search of their whereabouts. A moment of silence overwhelmed the men, who stared at each other: Bergmann with relief, Abram with anticipation. Just then Elsa, who had been taking a nap, rose off the living room couch and walked to the door, wondering who could be speaking to her husband in such a refined Berlin accent. As she approached from behind Abram, the man's face broke into a wider grin.

"*Meine* Elsa, *liebe* Elsa!" he exclaimed, eyes glistening. "You remember me from our school days, yes? I have something very important to give to you dearest Elsa." And in his hand, which he now extended to the sister, he held the postcard.

Thirteen

Kaiser at the Pump

I drifted around the Berg a lot that spring, wandering almost dreamlike as I gathered up my impressions of the place before I had to leave it. It was no longer a choice. The Kaiser was right: I had to go. I couldn't keep procrastinating and hiding out here any longer, "hanging on and getting older and avoiding decisions," as he said. But oh, the lanky flesh-filled peach-skinned Germans in their spring skirts with the white lace thongs crawling up their backs—they made it hard for any man to leave. Berlin was revving its engine for the long Nordic summer and now it ached me to say goodbye, so I responded by taking long meandering walks up and down the verdant hills of the Volkspark and sitting for hours at the sidewalk cafes on the corner of Sredzki and Kollwitzstrasse, soaking up the Berg's Napoleonic charm. From there I would cross Helmholzstrasse, hook down Stargaarderstrasse past the high-steeple red stone church drenched in sun, and under the U-bahn tracks into the Scandinavian Quarter. After a fast beer at the Blue Milk Canal I'd circle back via the Coal Cellar café and Mauerpark, reaching the tram tracks at Pappelallee that led me back to Kastanien, past the record and book shops, past the art supply stores, the Syrian kebab stands, past the three euro pizzas and four euro Thai plates and the posters advertising Baltic retreats and Sri Lankan gurus and multikulti sexshows. I went past all of it, I even passed Lotte's place and the corner wine bar at Zionskirch-platz before skirting around the drug dealers in Weinberg Park and continuing down the hill toward Mitte, where I would mix into the chic foreign crowds sitting out around Gorki's at Rosenthaler Platz and have another beer.

Most of all, in my nostalgic leaving of Berlin I got to pausing and gazing south down the baroque canyon of Rykestrasse, my favorite vista, where two rows of delicately sculpted peach-tone buildings ended at the austere, dark brick *Wasserturm*—the water tower around which the rest of the cozy wheel of Prenzlauer Berg turned—and hovering behind it, in clean ivory whiteness with a candy cane stem and metallic ball on top, the *Fernsehturm* at Alexanderplatz. That was my view, my Berlin. The Berg's beauty was all around me, it was circling me and I was circling it in what amounted to our final dance. Why had this city become more of a partner to me than any woman? I didn't have an answer. I was finally however starting to grasp, half a year after my break with Lotte, what the Kaiser had been trying to tell me: that women are in ascent and the best thing the disposable man can do is to get out of their way. Just leave. Women like Lotte, I realized, don't need a man. They need an assistant: a male who is eternally ready to put his needs second in order to help her, support her, push and bolster and buoy her, sympathize with her, sacrifice for her, suffer because of her and disburse emotions to her, but a male who, like a desert plant, requires only a drop of emotion in return. For a time I imagined I was that male: the running-around assistant to a generation of hysterical self-agitated women who refuse to let life's confusions and subtleties muddle or slow them. And I realized on those last salutary walks around the Berg that the Kaiser was right: A disposable man must accept himself for what he is. The sexes aren't at war, they're only at a sleepy stalemate and neither side knows whose move is next but what we do know is that women are studying harder, working longer, acting more and doubting less—and why shouldn't they now that they have disposable men at their sides to do their doubting for them? It's true we need a remedy. But that remedy won't be found in a society of men who go on bellyaching about the business of being men. I'm not whining, no, I'm only stating the facts and the fact is that the disposable man no longer has any arsenal at his disposal. He has dropped his armor like a suit on the floor and replaced it with terrycloth. There is no reservoir of fire for him to draw on and without fire a man is a threat to no one. He is a walking cul-de-sac, going nowhere. Stalled. Stuck. Inactive. Useless. The disposable man wants more but doesn't know what more is and knows less how to go about attaining it.

* * *

It was a balmy night in late May when I ended one of my walks at the *Schwarze Pumpe* to meet the Kaiser for a final drink. The Black Pump was a tidy corner pub on Choriner and Fehrbellinerstrasse that served the best chili in the Berg. A former coal production facility, it had very tall windows, towering ceilings, dark scuffed floorboards and an array of thick iron pipes mounted along the bar with heavy wooden seats attached to them. I was sitting on one of them, picking through a *Tageszeitung* and starting into my pint of Rothaus when Moritz the barman spoke.

"*Wie geht's dir denn*, Maxie?" he said in his deep-bellied tenor, lancing me with two hollowed out eyes.

"*Na ja*, things are alright, Moritz. A bit slow but at least spring is finally here."

"Yes, it is here. The question I want to know is when will summer arrive? I like to see Berliners being happy or at least pretending that they're happy."

"You're saying in Berlin everyone looks happy but no one is happy?" I gave Moritz a wink. "Not even in summer?"

"They try hard to convince you," he said, flushing out the beer mug in his hand. "Berliners are the most convincing people on Earth."

My gaze returned to the newspaper. The front page had a splashy photo of Nicolas Sarkozy, the French president, kissing German Chancellor Angela Merkel on the lips, or close to them, during a recent state visit to Berlin. Just then I heard the door creak open and saw the Kaiser stride in. He looked hunched, pressed down by the weight of his shoulders. He took off his bomber and fedora and hung them on a coat stand, then pulled up on the stool next to mine. "*Hallo* Moritz, *ein* Rothaus *bitte*," he said, drawing an unopened pouch of tobacco from his pocket. He tore the flap and started to roll one, and in a weary tone said, "I just talked to my mother."

"How is she?"

"Good. The usual. Nothing changes over there, you know how it is."

"Yeah." I picked up his tobacco to roll one.

"Bridge. TV shows. Walking the dog. I miss not being closer but the truth is I can't imagine ever going back."

"No one's asking you to, are they?"

"Maybe not, but part of me sometimes thinks I should. I don't know what it is, Max. My mom's a great woman. Grows a garden. Helps her friends. Reads from a mountain of books. She's generous, intelligent, great wit. Sometimes I wonder why I don't love her more than I do," he said, licking the paper and gliding it with his thumb and forefinger into a perfect rollup. Moritz served his beer and he took a sip.

"Five thousand miles is hard."

"Yeah," he said as a vacant glass-eyed look washed over his face. The Kaiser was already miles away, lost in deliberation, trying to remember or better, trying to understand. He took a long pull on his Rothaus which seemed to revive him. "But it's weird, Max, I'm really starting to like Rosa, you know, like, love her in a way. I mean I always wanted her, you know that, but now I'm actually starting to see a future with her. She's easy to be around, she treats me well, but more important is that I like the way she works. She wants to illustrate children's books, you remember, well the thing is she's gotten serious about it and now she's drawing non-stop and I can't take the pencil out of her hand. Remember she used to spend all her time in the cafes on Kastanien and Helmholz, smoking and drinking *Milchkaffee* and chattering that god awful high-pitched Spanish chatter with her friends? Well for some reason that's all over and now she's focusing, she's finding discipline and it's helping me get focused and disciplined too. We're actually getting work done, Max, we sit up there in the apartment and we each have our space and I'm telling you, the script's moving, it's finally happening."

"That's what I said, you just had to stay with—"

"Now don't get me wrong, I'm not saying I want to settle or marry or anything ridiculous like that, no, I'm not saying I want to get old in Spain, I mean shit, you've seen the old Spanish guys the way they sit out there on the *terrazas* with the football game playing loud inside and they've got their drink in hand, they're sprawled out in their wicker chair, shirtless, big round belly pushed up toward the sky and they're looking disconsolate, pointless, mourning the world through those heavy-lidded eyes. Spanish men are washed up like all the rest, Max, they're eating late breakfasts and reading yesterday's news—no, that ain't my future, that ain't my dream." The Kaiser tossed down the second half of his beer and signaled Moritz for another. "Thing is, maybe it's Germany that's got me whipped, I mean I know you're heading off quick here but—when you heading by the way?"

"Week after next."

"Right, shit, well I know you said you wanted to go and I'm glad you're going but you got me thinking I need to go somewhere myself, I don't know where, I'm just thinking I need to go. First I need to finish the damn script or maybe I need to go someplace else to finish it, shit, maybe I'll head to

Spain this summer with Rosa, to her place in Valencia, dig in on the coast, might be an idea what do you think?"

"It's a damn fine idea."

"Because I don't see a future for me in Berlin either, I mean yeah there's the whole mad arcane bohemian splendor thing going on and it's frivolous and dead serious at the same time which is why we like it, right? But you know as well as I do, Max, Germany is a godless country and the Germans are a godless race. Just look at their humor—they don't get it. Remember that girl I used to see, what was her name, Carolina, Cristal... Christiana! Yeah, remember what she told me, she said right off the bat, *Ich bin kein Clown,* she couldn't tolerate my jokes or anybody else's for that matter, but shit now that I think about it Christiana had a pretty fucked up family, actually now that I think about it every German I ever fucked had a fucked up family. What do you make of that, Max? Fucked up dads mostly, seriously fucked up relationships with their fathers, I'm talking mental abuse, beatings, incest. Really, why do you think that is?" But the Kaiser didn't give me a chance to respond, he was up on his high horse looking every bit the Kaiser and after a deep pull on his Rothaus he went on, "But apart from all that you know the best thing about German chicks, and you know this as well as me, Max, the best thing and the thing I'll miss the most is that they're first-night women. Yeah, if a German says she'll go out with you it means she'll fuck you, right? Better than the Brazilians who always want to wait until the second night, ain't that so? Now of course you have to be careful in this filthy town who you're fucking, I mean I don't know if I ever told you about that chick I pulled one night over at August Fengler. She was a busty one and we were drunk and I was riding home on the back of her bicycle around dawn, feeling the meat of her hips as she pedaled us through the streets and I knew I wanted her but at that point I didn't know what I was getting into, man, that shit got way over my head real fast because it turned out once we reached her flat and the door closed behind us I smelled something funny and I realized finally what I was smelling was the girl's ass. She hadn't wiped in days or something because the thing stank, the whiff of feces overwhelmed me, man, it was blowing me away but by then I didn't have a choice, I was stuck, you know, I mean what are you going to do, back out because of a dirty asshole? No, there was no turning back, like they say: 'If you're gonna get wet, get wet!' So right off the bat you know what I did? I stuck my goddamn fingers in her ass and cunt until she cried, *'Jawohl, jawohl!'* and when we finally got to fucking I must have passed out in disgust because the only thing I remember, man, was in the morning I woke up and looked down from the covers and saw this lash of blood across her thigh. She was bleeding, she was snoring, my fingers stank, I'd just fucked some chick with an unwiped ass and a ferocious period and man, Max, I cleared out."

"Nice one, Bruno."

The Kaiser started to roll one. After pausing just long enough to catch his breath, he continued, "It reminds me of that Kiwi I knew in New York, Flynn, I told you about Flynn the pussyhound, anyway Flynn warned me before I came to Europe, he said, 'Look out with the Germans, matey, by the third date they'll be pissin' and shittin' all over ya!' Now it ain't as bad as all that is it, Max, but I've got to say the undressing is a turnoff, I mean, for a German taking off her clothes means nothing, zilch, Germans get naked the first chance they get, it's some kind of expository syndrome or condition because everything just seems to come off in a piece and it doesn't mean a thing. That's because for Germans the dialogue is the foreplay. That's probably what you were missing with Lotte, maybe she wanted more of that conversation wetting her lips."

"Maybe so."

"Yeah probably so, probably so," the Kaiser said, "and anyway the conversation with them never ends so you're best not starting it, but fuck, what are we talking about German women for when you're going on a trip never to return, hot damn! You're finally getting out of here, Krumm, now what's the plan?"

"Me and the boys, Wayne and Robert and Alan, we're taking the train to Poznan and biking from there, then I'm on to Lithuania."

"Watch yourself in the East," said the Kaiser, turning suddenly serious. "The East is rough, you know that, Max, especially for us yids." He took a long drink and lit his cigarette from a candle, then sat for several moments in a deep meditative calm, shoulders slumped over the bar with his arms crossed. That was the Kaiser's art: to be able to suddenly turn off all the buzz and madness and just sit there enjoying the picture show playing inside his head. It was quiet for a while in that smoky air and auburn light of the *Schwarze Pumpe* when he said, "Speaking of the East, I ever tell you about the time I got arrested and taken hostage in Russia?"

"No."

"When Monica Lewinsky saved my life?"

"No." I started to roll one.

The Kaiser smiled, took a few drags to get his wind and washed it down with a quarter liter. "After college I was going across Siberia with my mother, see, we started in Vladivostok—"

"You and your mom went across Siberia?"

"Yeah, Max, will you let me tell the story? We went the summer I graduated, sort of a happy-graduation welcome-to-Siberia kind of trip. Anyway we took the train out of Vladivostok and let me tell you that is one crazy city: dead dogs floating in the harbor, mobsters trading money on the boulevards, Japanese guys fucking high-end whores in all the hotels. We were lucky to get out of there so we headed north and the first stop was Khabarovsk, then over the top of China and Mongolia until we got to Lake Baikal. Everything was going great with my mom and me, I was reading *War and Peace,* she was rereading *The Idiot* and what I remember us doing most was drinking. We drank like sailors. We'd buy a bottle of vodka at the train stops and drink it with the men in our cabin who were falling off their bunks drunk but it didn't matter none because there we were, my mom and me just reading and drinking and laughing with those bearish Russians as we headed across the Asian steppe, past end- less forest and rivers and those vast green wide-open spaces. It went on like that for days until we got close to Moscow and decided to go north through the old cities of the Golden Ring. That's when we came to Rostov Veliky. It had this old medieval monastery built out of wood with onion domes and spires and all that, they'd turned the place into a giant hotel so—"

"*Jungs was zu essen?*" Moritz bellowed from behind the bar as he set two fresh pints in front of us.

"What?" said the Kaiser with irritation. He'd finally found himself in the moment and didn't like being extracted from it. "No I don't want anything to eat, Max, you want anything to eat?"

"Chili."

"Okay, *zweimal* Chili," he said. Moritz retreated to the kitchen and the Kaiser relit his cigarette that had gone out somewhere along the Asian steppe. "Where was I—oh yeah, the monastery, so there we were in this little remote religious town and I forgot to tell you, Max, this was in the summer of '98 right after the Chechens blew up that hotel in Moscow, remember that, when they killed 300?"

"Yeah."

"Well I wasn't thinking about the Chechens or the bombs or any of it when I left my mom reading on the bed in our monastery hotel room and went out for a walk along the lake, Lake Nero, nice name for a lake, right? So anyway it was getting toward evening and lots of people were out promenading on the lakeshore which was nothing more than a dusty track along the water's edge, and I kept following the track along the lake for what must have been a mile or so until I stopped and looked back. The lakeshore was empty. All the people had gone home. It was idyllic out there, a perfect summer evening, so I took out my notebook and started to write, I was just taking notes, you know, standing alone out there at dusk scribbling in my pad when this long white van without any windows pulls up and a guy in a black beanie sticks his head out the passenger window and shouts something at me in Russian. I didn't understand the guy so I kind of flicked my head, you know, like, 'I don't understand what you're saying, man, *ne ponimayu,*' and turned back down to my notebook—"

The Kaiser took a long pull on his Rothaus and started clawing through his pouch looking for a filter. While he picked through the tobacco I could see his dark eyes burning as the scene replayed in his head, unfolding like it happened yesterday. Once he found the filter, he signaled Moritz for another beer and started to roll one, then continued.

"So the guy he says something else and this time I hear the word '*dokumenti*' and I realize, shit, I left my passport at the monastery, so I shrug and tell him in my scrap Russian, '*Ne govoryu po-russki,*' but as soon as I open my mouth BAM! the van door flies open and a huge guy in black fatigues and a black beanie with combat boots is suddenly walking toward me pointing a Kalashnikov at my chest. He puts the barrel right up on my heart, then grabs me by the arm and pulls me to the van, of course I can't argue with a six four guy pointing a machine gun at my chest so I step up inside the van where I see three other guys suited up in the same combat gear with Kalashnikovs on their laps. They're sitting on benches rigged around the van and in front of them I see three men that look kind of like me, they're dark and swarthy, they've got their legs spread and their hands behind their heads and they're pressed together one behind the other like a line of chickens, all in a row and folded together with their heads down." The Kaiser paused to light his cigarette and as he did, I noticed his hand was shaking. He went on, "So the soldier who grabbed me, he points at me to join the other guys and as I crouch down to sit, I sneak a look at the little dark man in front who lifts his head just enough that our eyes connect and I can see he's got fear like death written all over him. His eyes say, 'You've stepped in the shit, man,' and that's when the van door closed and the wheels began to roll and in the silence with my hands behind my head and my head pressed forward between my knees I began to take stock of just how bafflingly fucked I was. The first image that popped into my mind was Jackson and Travolta in *Pulp Fiction*, I ain't shitting you, Max, I thought, 'This is how it ends, this is what an execution looks and feels like, before it happens, before they off you in the trees and dump your body in Lake Nero,' and for five whole minutes that felt like forever, I'm thinking, 'It's over, this is all over, I'm going to die,' and I can feel my body shaking and I hear myself whimpering but the soldiers won't let me lift my head, all I can do is barely peek up and when I do I see their stone cold faces looking right through me as they cradle the black guns in their laps. No one said a word, the van was just rumbling along the dirt track in silence and I don't know what made me do it but just then I let the notebook slip out of my hand. I just let it fall open there on the floor between my legs. The notebook caught the soldiers' attention and one of them picked it up. He looked at it, turned it upside down, frowned, flipped through the pages, looked at it some more, unable to make out a word, then passed it to his partner. I lifted my head enough to see what was going on when one of the soldiers barked, 'Otkuda ty?' 'America,' I said, drawing out each syllable. I was desperate to speak. All I wanted them to do was to talk to me, make me human, because once you're human it's less easy to kill you. 'Amerikanski, New Yorki,' I said. 'Amerika?' said the soldier sitting closest to me. He looked down again at the journal, then threw it up front into the cab where the driver and a soldier sitting next to the driver studied it. I heard grumbling and a moment later the journal came flying back through the cab window, then it got batted around, from one soldier to the next, pages flapping like a big moth as the journal fluttered through the van until one of the soldiers laughed and in a deep voice silenced everyone with his shout: 'Amerika! Monica Leweeensky!' Suddenly the soldiers all erupted in chorus: 'Monica Leweeensky! Bill Clinton e Monica Leweeensky!' The impeachment had happened that winter, right, so there are these soldiers, they're rocking with laughter and slapping their knees and the machine guns are clanking and the journal is flying as the men keep shouting 'Monica Leweeensky!' with their big fleshy faces folded up in grins and I have to say, Max, it was only when the laughter broke and they looked at me for the first time like I was a member of the human species that my heart stopped hammering through my chest and my lungs stopped convulsing and I thought I might just get out of that van in one piece. I wanted to keep things in my favor so I jabbered, 'Home New Yorki, wife, baby, New Yorki. Mama monastery, passport monastery,' and I pointed back in whatever direction back was because I could see through the front window of the van that we were no longer near any lake, we were on pavement now, traveling through the town, it was dark out and suddenly the soldiers in the van were pressing me for money. They held out their big gorilla paws in that universal language which said: *Pay*. I showed them my pockets which were empty. I had nothing on me, not even my *dokumenti*, all I had was that rotten word *monastery* so I said it again and again and watched their frowns grow heavy with disappointment as the van drove on in silence. For the next half hour we circled the town, passing checkpoints where the driver would stick his head out and chat for a moment with soldiers who were stationed there, holding guns, looking for Chechens. They gabbed like they had all evening to gab as I sat, silent, hands around my head, head to the floor, waiting. Finally the van wheeled up at the monastery and the door slid open. One of the soldiers pushed me out and as I left the van I glanced back at the three dark guys sitting behind me with their heads still down. They didn't look up, the poor bastards, they didn't have a pricey monastery to get out at or an Amerikanski passport or anything else to save them, and I don't know and don't want to know what happened to those three little dark Chechen-looking dudes because it wasn't going to be good. When I stepped out into the muggy evening air I saw the word 'OMOH,' the name of Russia's paramilitary police, written in big yellow letters across a soldier's back. So the door closes and the van tears away but literally two steps before I reach the monastery gate another white van screeches to a halt and a guy in a black beanie sticks his head out the window and the van door flies open, but that's when I shoot them a look, a gesture so clear and insane as I point at the van still in sight that the combat man understands, he nods, gets back in and the vehicle leaves. When I finally return to the room my mom is lying on the bed, novel in hand, she says, 'Why were you gone so long?' and that's when I start shaking, Max, my voice is trembling and I tear open a pack of cigarettes and—where's our goddamn chili? Moritz, chili *bitte!*"

"Jesus, Bruno."

"So all I'm saying is: Watch it in the East. Get your business done then get your ass out."

"Yeah."

"Come down to Spain, Rosa and I'll show you around the coast."

"I might do that." A visit with the Kaiser on the Mediterranean sounded fine. I started to roll one.

"We'll set you up with one of her Valencianas, how's that for sweetener? Sangria pouring in the streets. Ocean and mountains everywhere you look. Just get your balls back, Max. We can't all be disposable forever, can we? Hey Moritz!" the Kaiser shouted, finishing his Rothaus and signaling for another. "Is our chili coming or what?"

"*Jetzt! Kommt gleich!*" said Moritz as he hurried toward us with two hot bowls balanced on round wood trays. Finally, with food in front of us, the Kaiser and I bent our heads and in the bar's muted light we forgot about Siberia, forgot about writing and violence and women and balls and all of it, forgot about everything except for the beans and the hot saucy ground beef that was staring us in the face.

Fourteen

Josey Gets Her Boots

Yakutsk, 1942

It was the first day of February, as the women were taking their morning soup and wrapping themselves tightly
in work garments before the lorry came, when a guard burst
into the barrack and ordered Josephine to step outside.

"You have been called to the commissar's office," the
guard said. "You are excused from your duties for the morning. Go immediately."

Blood rushed to Josephine's face. She walked quickly over
the frozen road into Yakutsk, stumbling several times on the
flaps of leather that she had affixed to the soles of her shoes,
which were cumbersomely peeling off. Josephine entered the
commissar's bureau and greeted Captain Prikov, who stared
at her coldly and told her to wait outside the office door until she was called. She could feel the warm air coming up
from beneath the commissar's door; they had plenty of coal
in there and the fire never went out. Josephine would have
been happy to spend all day sitting on the chair outside the
office but just then she heard a shout. "Comrade Grunefeld!"
the voice yelled through the door.

"Yes," she said, standing, opening the door and closing
it quickly behind her. She walked in short fast steps to the
commissar's desk and bowed slightly with her head. "Comrade Commissar."

The commissar was a very short man with heavy jowls,
a moustache and cloudy, unclean eyes. He inspected Josephine, taking in her appearance from head to foot like an

animal sizing up its prey. "Comrade Grunefeld," he repeated, and a whiff of vodka blew across the desk.

"Yes, Comrade Commissar."

"A very interesting package has arrived from the United States of America bearing your name. Have you heard something of it?"

"No, Comrade Commissar, not a word."

"And you wouldn't know who the package is from, would you?"

"No, Comrade Commissar. I have a sister living in America so perhaps it comes from her," she said, careful not to betray the slightest emotion.

"Hmmm.... yes," groaned the commissar. "Your sister must be a good investigator to find you all the way out here in Yakutsk, don't you think, Comrade Grunefeld?"

"Yes, Comrade Commissar, I imagine she worked very hard to find her dear sister."

"Her dear sister, her dear sister—if she were such a dear sister then why did she leave for that dogshit-eating empire of capitalists, America, tell me that, Comrade Grunefeld! Why does every capitalist *zhid* filth have a relative in America?"

"I don't know, Comrade Commissar."

"No, of course you don't," the commissar intoned, staring down at his plump fingers. A silence passed before he looked up and shot her a glare. "Our officers searched the package thoroughly, Comrade Grunefeld, and judged it is in the interest of the prisoner to receive it."

"Oh thank you, Comrade Commissar!"

"You are a fortunate prisoner, you know that don't you?"

"Yes, Comrade Commissar," said Josephine, "but no more fortunate than many of my comrades. I am only trying to serve my nation and survive the winter in my new home Yakutsk."

The commissar stood up from his chair and walked slowly around the desk. Josephine felt soaked in a blanket of vodka as he stopped behind her chair, laid his fat hands on her shoulders and leaned down with his breath close to her ear.

"There are more comfortable ways to survive winter in Yakutsk, Comrade Grunefeld," he whispered. "You must know those ways by now."

Josephine struggled not to shudder as she felt the commissar's fleshy fingers exploring the area between her neck and shoulders. She remained still, absolutely calm, as though no more than a fly had touched upon her back. Her silence enraged the commissar, who snatched his hand away. "Because if you don't know these ways then it is time you got to know them," he shouted. "You will stay warmer and have better food to eat and less hours to work and you won't have to wait months for a dogshit package to arrive from the United States of—"

The commissar's voice broke off. He returned to his desk and faced the wall with his back to Josephine. Then he opened a large wooden cabinet and pulled a box down from one of the middle shelves. He scoffed at the lettering before tossing the package on the desk. Josephine picked it up. Her heart stirred as she felt the box's weight.

"Understand me, Comrade," he said, and the fermented odor added a sharpness to his words. "If you want to survive Yakutsk—if you want to return one day to see that sister of yours, when the war is over and the People of the Glorious Soviet States of Russia have triumphed over Nazi Europe and that bastard land America—you will need more than a pair of boots to do it!"

"I understand, Comrade Commissar. Thank you, Comrade Commissar," she said with a slight bow and walked hurriedly from the office.

The barrack was empty when Josephine returned. At any moment the midday lorry would arrive to take her to the forest. Josephine had been dreaming of this day for months and knew that in an instant the pleasure would be over so she savored every sound, every touch. Sitting on her cold bunk, she untied the string around the package, carefully undid the brown paper wrapping, lifted off the lid and with her eyes closed, placed her hands inside the box. She could already smell the leather's sweet, oily fragrance before her fingers met the smooth folds. She felt around inside the boots, touching a fur that was softer than any she had ever known. A piece of paper had been stuffed into the left boot. Elsa wrote that she was pregnant, expecting the child in spring, and that Abram had gotten a job with an architecture firm. "Josey dearest," Elsa wrote, "You are so strong and you must remain strong. The war will end and we will be together soon. With greatest love, your sister Elsa."

Josephine pulled the boots out of the box and put them on her lap. Her mind returned then to that summer day on the *kolkhoz,* in Barnaoul, when an NKVD guard had stopped her on the roadside and asked, "Tell me, Comrade, how come all the other women cry and you do not?"

"Oh sir, you know the proverb," she told him. "Moscow does not believe in tears."

But now Josephine believed in tears and she believed in miracles as well. She longed to hug her sister and Abram, to throw her arms around the neck of Valentin Bergmann and to kiss Albert Einstein, oh! to press a thousand kisses on the gentle brilliant face of Herr Professor Doktor Einstein for he had done the thing she imagined it was not possible to do. Yes, the Herr Doktor had done it, she cried. He had saved her life.

* * *

That winter, fueled with a new sense of hope, Josephine wrote letter after letter in which she repeated the same request: Would authorities grant her permission to travel west to fetch her father, Anton Isaakovich Grunefeld, from the North Ural Work Camp, and bring him to join her in Yakutsk? She wrote to Stalin. She wrote to Molotov. She even addressed her petition to Beria, the monstrous head of the Secret Police. Finally, in April, a guard approached Josephine and summoned her again to the commissar's. This time, however, it was not the short, fat, vodka-smelling creature who received her but a mere voice speaking through the transmitter line.

"Comrade Grunefeld this is the Secret Police don't repeat just say yes."

"Yes."

"You will report tomorrow evening at ten o'clock at room two zero two just say yes."

"Yes."

"There will be an officer waiting for you with particulars about the case of Anton Isaakovich Grunefeld just say yes."

"Yes."

When Josephine showed up the next evening she received a telegram: The authorities had approved Anton Grunefeld's journey alone to Yakutsk. Josephine waited days, then weeks, and when her father finally stepped off the boat she hardly recognized him. He was bony, fleshless, discolored. His eyes loomed out of deep caves on his face. Josephine wept when she saw him and she wept still more that night when, with the permission of the guards, she took her father for a drink at the Miner's Club and he recounted, word for memorable word, his interrogation in Svertlovsk where he had been deported after the family's arrest and separation in Kovno:

"Comrade Anton Isaakovich, I see you are Ukrainian by birth," the Jr. Lt. Filip Shurkalov had begun.

"That is correct, Lieutenant," I responded.

"And you moved in 1910 to Berlin to pursue studies in engineering?"

"That is correct, Lieutenant."

"Yet you later resettled in your wife's home city of Kovno to open the Lithuanian German Technical Trade Company where you sold water, heating and other electrical parts, yes?"

"Yes, Lieutenant."

"You zhids move around too much from place to place, Anton Isaakovich. Don't you know where you belong?"

"I needed to support my family."

"Yes, quite right. And the annual turnover from your store, Anton Isaakovich, can you remember what it was?"

"About half a million litas."

"You were the owner of a shop that had been already nationalized and your annual turnover was... let me correct you, Anton Isaakovich, it was one million three hundred twenty seven thousand litas. That is what our records show," said the junior lieutenant.

"It never reached more than half a million, Lieutenant, I can assure you—"

"Then either our records are wrong or you are lying to us, and our records are never wrong, Anton Isaakovich. Do you plead guilty to the accusation that you violated Article 35 of the Criminal Code of the USSR?"

"Comrade Lieutenant, I admit that I owned a shop and used a hired workforce—"

"You did not use them—you exploited them, Anton Isaakovich, you exploited a hired workforce. You are the very zhid capitalist scum without regard for the suffering of the common man that the Union of Soviet Socialist Republics will eradicate! How

131

many workers exactly did you exploit?"

"Fifteen."

"What contacts did you keep in Germany?"

"I had business with two small companies until 1933."

"Did you maintain commercial contacts in the USSR during that time?"

"Yes, I went to Moscow in 1932, '34 and '36."

"For what purpose?"

"To buy ball bearings, Lieutenant."

"Ball bearings?"

"Yes, ball bearings."

The Jr. Lt. Filip Shurkalov didn't know just then what to make of me so he sat in silence. After ruffling the pages in front of him, clearly displeased with the answers he had received, Shurkalov concluded the interrogation. "Anton Isaakovich, have you received any awards, medals or weapons from the Soviet government?"

"No."

"Have you served in the Red Army, the Red Guard or partisan groups?"

"No."

"Have you served in the White counterrevolutionary forces?"

"No."

"Have you participated in gangs, counterrevolutionary organizations or other mutinies?"

"No."

"Alright then, Anton Isaakovich, you may leave. I see you are a man who makes unwise decisions. But you and your family were fortunate to be arrested and deported when you were because two weeks later the Germans entered Kovno and shot every zhid they could find. They would not have given you the chance to reform and correct your thinking the way we are doing now."

A musician strummed mournfully on the strings of a balalaika at the back of the Miner's Club as Josephine wiped the smear of vodka from her lips and wept quietly. She had no way of knowing, and strongly doubted, whether her ill brother Bubi was alive. The day of their separation still haunted her. But now, hearing her frail beloved father opposite her recount his story of incarceration and survival, she rejoiced that they could now at last endure the war's hardships together. She placed her hand on her father's wrist. It was cold, brittle, like touching a branch. But as she gazed into the long and faithful lines on Anton's face, she had a premonition that the worst of their suffering was behind them.

* * *

Due to his diminished age and condition, Anton Isaakovich was spared the kind of harsh physical labor that his daughter performed at Yakutsk Workers Camp. He instead took a job cataloguing books at the city's library of foreign literature, which was housed in a small church on the outskirts of town. In the summer of 1942, Josephine too escaped the treachery of the woods when she was transferred to the city laboratory close to her father's work. Her job consisted of testing patients' blood, pumping acids from their stomachs and performing various other crude analyses using the homespun implements available. One time, Zavjalov, the head of the Secret Police for the whole of Yakotia Republic, entered the laboratory to have his stomach acids tested. Josephine searched for the widest hose she could find and stuck it down his throat and afterwards she asked if he would also like to have some tea. Zavjalov took out his revolver and without a word placed it on the table—his way of thanking her for the service.

One autumn evening after she left the laboratory, Josephine was on her way to see her father when she stopped at a cellar shop to buy a sandwich and a man with trembling hands approached her.

"Can I please sit with you?" he said.

"Of course," she replied.

"I want to know your name because if I go now to the front, if I die, just like that, I want to know your name. I want to be able to think of you, just like that," he stammered.

"Are you going to the front?"

"Yes."

"Do you have any cigarettes?"

"No."

"Do you have bread?"

"No."

"Come with me, I will give you what you need," Josephine said, and she bought the man two packets of cigarettes and a loaf of bread. Then she told him her name. The man thanked her with piteous eyes and as he turned to leave, it occurred to Josephine that in the Soviet Union one is born first a slave and only second a man. She was grateful that her first year in Yakutsk had passed and that she no longer knew fear. Starvation. Freezing. Imprisonment. Execution. None of it meant a thing to her any longer. Unlike the desperate man being sent to die at the front, the future did not concern Josephine. She did not steal. She did not lie. She did not kill. She knew the war would one day end, and, with it, a new freedom she could not right now imagine would begin.

FIFTEEN

THE POLAND TRIP

Warta River, Poland, 2009

I nearly missed the train that high June morning when we set off with our bikes for Poland. I'd stayed up late the night before packing, cleaning, fiddling around Eduardo's apartment, too anxious to sleep, and when I looked out at the gray Berlin morning I groaned. It was dark and drizzly, another accursed unsummerlike day in the German capital and there wasn't a bone in me that wanted to stay there any longer so I locked the apartment, mounted my saddle bags and coasted down the Allee. I blew past the early crowds shopping at Alexanderplatz, continued under Jannowitzbrücke and pedaled the long straight path of Heinrich-Heine-Strasse into Kreuzberg until I reached the Landwehrkanal. Few things in Berlin provided a quieter pleasure than watching the Kreuzberg swans linger picturesque in the murky, copper-colored waters of the canal. Rusted iron barges were moored alongside the grass embankment where weeping willows looked majestic in their dense summer green; willows that, as Joseph Roth once put it, "were not created by God at the same time as the other trees, like the hazelnuts and the apple trees, but only after He had decided to allow people to die." Yes, the Berlin summer morning was gray and cold and felt like piss but nonetheless I rode with an invincible air up on my olive-green Dutch Gazelle bicycle that I called the Junker. I had loaded the Junker with provisions: cutlery, a pot, an axe, a tent, a sleep sack, books, clothes, maps, food, grappa and tobacco, all of it strapped on and bulging off in a mishmash survivalist style as if I were embarking on a voyage across the Gobi Desert rather than a stoners' weekend idyll in Poland. Traveling with me, tucked safely in the pages of a book, wrapped in layers of plastic to keep the wet out, was the object that mattered most: Aunt Josephine's postcard. It was my passport, my ticket, for this journey into the past.

In one final reminiscence of Kreuzberg, I crossed the bumpy cobblestones of the Admiralbrücke and looped through the quiet Graefekiez. The minutes were dangling close to noon as I stopped for an espresso at Café Avril before circling back to Kottbusser Damm. I sped past the men with thick moustaches and women dressed in headscarves and all the criers shouting out prices for figs and melons at the Turkish market, then I cut east back along the canal pedaling through sweet-smelling plumes of smoke that billowed out from the groupings of African dope dealers who stood with yellowed eyes in Görlitzer Park. I biked past the bustling cafes on Schlesischestrasse, across the Oberbaumbrücke with its sweeping view of industry along the Spree River, and made one last mad kilometer dash along the graffiti-covered remains of the Berlin Wall before I reached the Ostbahnhof. I got there just as Easy Wayne was stuffing the last of a McDonald's rib sandwich into his mouth while Robert and Alan stood smoking at the station entrance. At four minutes to noon we shouldered our bikes up the stairs to Platform 1, hoisted them on to the Warsaw Express, and soon were clanking east.

The train made many early stops as it left the concrete sprawl of Berlin's outlying districts behind, gathering pace as it bounded into the countryside. For a time rain lashed the windows, then a bright sun emerged and sharp light poured in as we rushed through bright yellow fields of sunflowers and corn shimmering between long, unbroken corridors of pines. We had a coupe to ourselves and were already feeling giddy from the grappa when we crossed the marshy Oder River into Poland and Alan locked the door. He drew the curtain closed, pulled a crumpled envelope out of his breast pocket and said, "Rob, hand me the book you're reading will you?" Robert closed his dog-eared copy of Steinbeck's *The Wayward Bus* and handed it to Alan, who put old Steinbeck on his lap and dumped a thimble-sized mound of powder on the cover. Alan couldn't cook. He didn't own a tent. His contribution to the journey was limited to those two pungent sparkling grams of blow he had acquired from his Croatian dealer, Milo, who worked at a roughneck Slav bar called the Blue Apple on the eastern fringe of the Berg. It cost Alan 70 euros a gram but Milo called it "top shit" and raved it was "the best from Zagreb." So there we were, speeding toward Poznan as Alan cut the powder with his Alliance Member Visa card and Easy Wayne fished around his wallet for a U.S. twenty but came up short.

"All I got's euros," said Wayne.

"Euros won't do, that shit's plastic," said Alan. "We need an Andrew J. Who's got greenbacks?"

"Hang on, ah think ah got a dirty greenback. Yeh, ah jost got tips playing for the tourists," said Robert pulling out a crisp twenty dollar bill. He rolled it up tight into a cylinder and handed it to Alan, who held the bill ceremoniously between his thumb and forefinger like a delicate wine glass as he proposed a toast.

"Fellas I just want you to know I'm glad—glad we're on this trip together, that we're doing this together. Here's to the Warsaw Express." Alan lowered his face to old Steinbeck and drew loudly through his good right nostril.

"Alright alright!" said Easy Wayne, taking the Andrew J and going down for a hit. After him it was my turn, then Robert, and we had a few more go-arounds as the bright forests glistened and the golden fields blew past. The sun was glowing on our faces, permeating everything the way a summer sun should and we'd have held on to that moment if we could—held it with anticipation and hope and the thinking that we were free, bound for *someplace,* to make *something* happen, anything at all. It all seemed once more possible as we gazed out euphoric on the orange-tiled rooftops of the Polish homes and farmhouses bathed in the blistering afternoon light. "Shit boys, to stop feeling, stop talking, stop thinking anything at all, that's what it's about," said Wayne and we rode in that collective stupor until we reached Poznan.

The first thing we did in the city was ride up to the citadel above town where we sat down in a field of tall grass, surrounded by the rusted remains of World War II tanks and busted Polish aircraft, and smoked a bifter. As it got on close to evening we pedaled south, clearing the city outskirts until all of a sudden we found ourselves on a heavy mud track along the Warta River where men in army fatigues with cigarettes stuck to their lips shot us hostile squinting looks as they stood fishing in the reeds. The trail got hard to follow as darkness crept in and, with it, a sense that something ominous awaited us. Finally, in the last of the dusk we came upon a meadow. There were crickets jumping and the sound of trains thundering past as we pitched camp and made a fire. Robert pulled out the vodka, Wayne rolled a bifter and maybe it was the blow from earlier or maybe all that grappa but a miserable sullen air got hold which stopped us communicating—stopped us wanting or having anything to say at all. Wayne and Robert and Alan and me, we called ourselves friends, it's what we genuinely considered ourselves to be, but what we were really was the implied company of men. We were mysteries to each other; mysteries that we didn't understand and didn't want or need to understand. All we wanted was to share this solemn getting older feeling—to finish, one could say, executing our youths—and around the fire that night the silence made it painfully clear how useless but also how natural it felt to be in all this disposable company of disposable men.

* * *

In the morning Easy Wayne was the first to rise so he lit the stove and boiled coffee. We drank vodka with our muesli and Robert rolled a bifter so by half ten we were feeling, as Wayne put it, "pretty alright." We packed camp and charged out on our bikes through the woods and plains. The sun was bright, the fields spectacularly lit with color as we crossed meadows throbbing with butterflies and wildflowers. You could see the Warta River through the birch trees flowing wide and brown, swirling with eddies as the breeze whipped along it. My bike, the Junker, was weighed down with all that gear but still I managed to pedal it over the dirt path, riding it the way my grandfather Abram used to ride: straight-backed, unhurried, with a steady clicking sound through the woods. I felt I was pedaling into my past, to the place my ancestors wanted me to go, and as I rode under the cool forest canopy with Easy Wayne and Alan up ahead and Robert some distance behind, I recalled the rides I had taken many years ago with Abram when he sat up high on his junker and I sat on mine as we pedaled during long hot summer afternoons through the eucalyptus groves near his home in Menlo Park, not far from Aunt Josey's.

There were days, remembering back, when I didn't even think we would make it out to ride at all on account of Abram's indigestion. He'd be sitting at the dining room table after lunch sipping tea from a teaspoon and emitting belches. I remember how he would take a sugar cube from the saucer on the table, bite the cube in half, put one half back in the saucer and the other half on his spoon, then dip his spoon in the tea and slurp the tea through the filter of the sugar as it melted brown around his lips. The routine made his wife Minnie furious. "Abram, you have no regard for hygiene!" she scolded, but Abram ignored the shrunken woman with the sour face who was his wife and instead leaned back in his seat, released a series of short, frog-like burps, then reached into his chest pocket for the small tin box that contained his pills. Abram was always eating the pills, before lunch and after lunch and all day long he was eating them because the pills calmed the burn that was raging in his chest and once the burn was calmed Abram would laugh, at times uproariously. The laughter came funneling out through his big canine teeth as he laughed about life in its comic proportions and laughed about death as well. I remember as a teenager once asking him, "Grandpa, are you afraid of death?" Abram laughed. "What is there to fear?" he said. "Death is not a period, it's just a comma. It's all in Martin Buber. There I find everything I need. Continuity, Maximilian, life is about continuity and it is about form."

I didn't know precisely what he meant so I followed Abram into his study after lunch and stood with him beneath the faces gazing down at us from the wall. Some were portraits drawn in ink, others were photographs in black and white. There was the man with the long bony face and chin, his hair neatly matted, who stared with sharp eyes into the distance and his name was Pasternak. Another had a thick bristly moustache and tall forehead, that was Nietzsche. The one with the sly smile who wore round frameless glasses and had tight leathery skin was Hesse. And next to him was a wild-looking man with a tall square forehead, fiery eyes and long sideburns that grew down past his jaw, whose name was Pushkin. Finally, the man on the wall with the most ordinary appearance—quiet-looking, with glasses, graying hair and a pair of gentle questioning eyes—he was Chekhov. These were the men who, along with Buber, constituted Abram's society. They were his friends, his partners, his allies and closest company. The conversations he held with them were chatty and unending and they filled up the long warm California existence of Abram's later years.

Abram had moved to the Bay Area after retiring as an architect and he brought his third wife, Minnie, with him. (His second wife, a Russian dancer he met shortly after Elsa, died tragically young from cancer.) Now you might not think an old war-scarred Jew from Smolensk would find his home in the mad materialistic rush that was Silicon Valley in the 1980s, but Abram did. He studied Homo californicus with boundless amusement and sympathetic fascination, all the while sustaining the same basic activities that had brought him pleasure since he was a child, that is to say he drew, he read, he played chess and he bicycled. Abram loved his bicycle. He was like an orchestral maestro sitting poised up high above the wheels with his old legs churning and his memory wheel spinning and the junker carrying him forward through a symphony composed of whistling and bird song. Abram would delay our rides for as long as possible in order to digest his lunch, sitting cross-legged, European-style, hands in lap, while he interrogated me with questions about the friends I had and the classes I was studying and the sports I was playing and the instruments I was learning, and he laughed about it all because Abram's laughter was his sign of love. He was erupting in burps and laughter, his sharp teeth were showing with his brown crescent eyes merrily folding in on themselves until suddenly he stood, rubbed the bristles of his peppery moustache, cinched his belt tight around his waist and pronounced: "Max, it is time to ride."

It was like the crack of a gunshot signaling the start of a race as we hurried out the door past Minnie before she could nag us in. We'd descend the stairs to the garage where the junkers were waiting and within minutes we were out on the bright street, Abram pedaling in front and swerving carefully to avoid the seed pods with the prickly points that had fallen from the trees. He chided me when I didn't avoid the pods and he chided me when I rode too close on Minnie's junker. "Stay behind!" he shouted and I would keep my distance until we reached the leafy mansions in Atherton where our pace slowed and I could finally ride up alongside him to receive my lesson. There was always a lesson on our bicycle journeys and Abram normally took things from the top starting with the Greeks, then moving to Spinoza, the Renaissance, the Enlightenment, Goethe, Dostoevsky, Camus. Abram lived engulfed in history and literature and while pedaling he was unstoppable in his reflections on the past; he even once talked with me about the cuckolding and about his early attraction to his sister-in-law in the period before the war, which ended when he and Elsa fled west from Prague and Josephine fled north "because she couldn't abandon her father or her invalid brother" in Kovno, Abram said, "and because she couldn't bear the thought of—"

"Of what?" I asked.

Abram's voice stopped. I waited for him to continue because I sensed an importance in the words he was not telling me. We biked together for a long time in silence, letting the breeze blow away his words as though it might also blow away the shadows of the past. But as I rode up close Abram must have seen the doubt still in my eyes. By then we'd left the mansions and were deep among the eucalyptus groves near Stanford University when he turned his head in my direction and asked sharply:

"Max, what is it you want to do?"

"Do?"

"What do you want to do with your life?"

"I don't know," I answered because at sixteen it was the

truth. A long silence passed as Abram, sitting erect with his pigeon-perfect view on the world, navigated the junker between the trees. All I could hear was the wind in my face and the sound of the chain clicking. He spoke again:

"When I was young, little more than your age, architecture seemed to me a dull, uninteresting subject. It was orderly and arranged and practical and I was none of those things. I wanted to be an artist, an actor. I didn't know what I wanted to be. Even in Berlin I didn't know, and then in Prague—"

Abram slowed his pedaling and stopped under the shade of a large eucalyptus. I stopped with him and we stood leaning on the junkers.

"In Prague?"

"In Prague I had to make a decision. From Prague we went to London and then the war came and so many dreadful things but what I want to tell you, Max, is that by then I had found my work in life. I intended to be an artist and instead became an architect. It wasn't what I wanted or planned but in the end it was the thing that gave me *form*." A gentle breeze was blowing through the eucalyptus grove as Abram adjusted his glasses, looked at me with a composed expression, and said: "What will be your office, Max? What is the thing that will give you form?"

I stared back, a blank response. "I don't know."

"You asked me what I think about death," he went on, "but I'll tell you: I do not think about death. I think about continuity. Life is continuous. Through birth and death flow infinite time—continuous unbroken *time*. You know the story, Max, of how my father and mother ended, in Riga, shot in the mud by the Nazis on their march into the woods. It is terrible that I was not there to help them survive, but I am consoled by the fact that, to me, Father is not dead. He has never been dead for the reason that I continue to see and to speak with Mikhail every day. Our conversations have grown richer with the years. Father is a link continuing into the past and you are a link that continues into the future. I am linked in time, Max: I am saved by continuity. Death concerns me little. What concerns me is life because life requires form. Without form we are formless. It is for this you must discover what you want to do."

"I don't know what I want to do."

"What is it you *like* to do?"

I stared at Abram, silent, unable to suppress the sudden panic I was feeling.

"Let me ask this, then," he persisted, his brown almond eyes boring through me as dapples of sunlight filtered through the leaves and danced across his bald pate. "As a wiser man once put it: What is it you think you like to do, which you *can* do?"

I stood there, frozen still, without an answer to give my grandfather. For as long as I could remember I had had no answer—for sixteen years I had lived without an explanation of myself. My thoughts were a stampede, my blood swam hot. I choked in search of a response, gasping, clinging, then like a tide drawn out suddenly by some mysterious force, the uncertainty receded. I saw a child standing before an infinite slate holding on to a small piece of chalk.

"I like to write."

Abram released me from his scrutinizing gaze and burst into laughter. It was an uproarious laugh as he threw his head back, rocking on his feet. "Marvelous!" he exclaimed. "So write!"

Then he climbed back up on his junker and I climbed back on mine and we pedaled off fast for home because it was getting late and he didn't want Minnie to start her worrying and her shaking. I was careful to keep my distance behind Abram, watching his weathered body sit up high and balanced and free as his old legs churned and he cut a cool path through the autumn afternoon.

* * *

Around midday we veered off the river trail and stopped at a village store where Alan and Wayne loaded the saddle bags with beer and Robert rolled a bifter. "Ah'll jost get us a little feller on the go," he said so we stood in the parking lot outside the market and smoked the bifter under a sparkling blue Polish sky, then got back on our rigs. We roared out through the woods, pedaling into fields of wheat and bronze shimmering barley as Wayne, who was very high, shouted, "I like it! I like it! Every little goddamn thing!" and soon we liked the whole goddamn thing so much we decided to take another break. We dumped the bikes, sat down on a small embankment overlooking the Warta and pulled out our pouches of tobacco and our bottles of grappa. We were ruined and we thrilled in the ruining. There was something ecstatic in all that gesticulation of manhood. Our ruin aped our manhood. It mocked it, distorted it, anesthetized it, and with our ambitions prostrate we let the soup of oratory take us.

"It's been a steady intake," said Alan.

"Yeh," said Robert.

"Someone get a fatty on the roll. Anybody seen my filters?"

"Yeah Rob, make us a righteous salad," said Wayne, tossing him a piece of hash from his pouch. "It's only noon, fucking genius."

"I can't believe how—"

"Perfect," said Wayne.

"Yeah, perfect," said Alan.

"It's perfect, it is," Robert repeated.

"Perfect right now, like this."

"With incredible weather—"

"High summer—"

"Absolutely fucking perfect—"

"June on the river."

We looked out over the Warta flowing wide and green beneath the embankment. Sunlight rained through the poplars and laurels as the day paused in a splendid silence. Easy Wayne, cross-legged on the grass, broke the quiet.

"You know what's nice is we haven't had a hill yet," he said.

"Hmm."

"I mean, you know, riding up a hill with all this shit would be—"

"Yeh it's pretty flat in't it," said Robert.

"It's a rolling plain," said Alan.

"Exactly, I mean shit, it's just flat—"

"Hmm."

"Someone seen my papers?"

"Because man, when I was biking in the Pyrenees it was a motherfucker sometimes, you know, where you're just going uphill—"

"I thought you went *around* the Pyrenees—"

"for forty five minutes—"

"Hmm."

"So it's like, great, now I'm going uphill again because what you're really doing is downhilling for five then up-hilling for forty five and it's like, goddamn, you never—"

"It ain't pretty."

"Get a break, you know, but hey this is excellent."

"Hmm, jost watching the river go by," said Robert.

"Serious river, be nice for a dip," I said.

"Ah wouldn't swim in it none though, I reckon it must be pretty polluted ain't it."

"What, you think you can't—"

"Contaminated with the chemical plant yeh—"

"Fucking industry."

"Nothing like the five year plans to destroy nature. Just get it fucking done."

Robert lit the bifter and handed it to Wayne, then said, "Ah remember when ah was in Armenia. Them old factories was frightenin', like some plant the town grew op around and now the plant's closed down but you go there and it's like out of Gotham City, big tower stacks—"

"Yeh."

"With smoke flyin' out of them—"

"Yeh."

"But jost built in some fokin', ah don't know, some ragged fokin' way."

"Goddamn now where's my tobacco?" said Alan.

The bifter made its way around as Easy Wayne somehow got on the subject of Mount Everest and the German climber, Reinhold Messner, who summited without using oxygen and walked right past a team of Japanese climbers dying in a storm.

"Carried his shit the whole way alone," said Wayne.

"Alone?"

"Yeh, alone, carrying his own shit without oxygen, Messner, he's the hard core, the hardest core—"

"Without oxygen—"

"Carrying his own shit—"

"Up Everest alone—"

"They say every step is grueling, there's just no oxygen up there, none at all—"

"Human tenacity in't it, I mean."

"Well that's what it is."

"Like that thing in National Geographic—"

"It's the challenge—"

"About that Dutch dude, or Swedish dude, you know, who went—"

"Now who's got a light?"

"Out in fucking Siberia for like a year or something, just surviving, you know, somehow in minus twenty—"

"No way I could do it or want to do it but still I can imagine you could do it—"

"Maybe he jost did it for the buzz."

"Yeh, knowing you can push yourself, sort of like what we're doing out here, at least in principle," said Alan.

"Haha!" Easy Wayne took a rip. "Like how much can you drink and smoke and still stay on the bike."

Robert leaned back in the grass. Soon Alan did too, then Wayne and I did the same and within minutes our crew was asleep, spread out in the sun with the high cottony clouds overhead and the river gurgling past. It was the good part of an hour before Robert awoke looking for a smoke.

"What's that, someone got my baccy?"

Wayne sat up and tossed Robert one of three pouches he'd been hoarding in his pants. "Sorry bro I had it."

"I heard them papers rustlin', I can always hear 'em rustlin', even in my sleep I hear 'em. What we say to gettin' a bifter on the go?"

"Alright then let's move, it's getting late," said Wayne.

"I hear you, let's jost have us a little feller before we leave." Robert started to roll one and suddenly Alan bolted upright.

"I was in a deep dream, fellas, something strange," he said. "Wiebke and me were there but somehow she was the man and I was the woman."

"What you talkin' about Alan, Wiebke your old kraut nag from way back?" said Robert, licking the paper as he twisted up the bifter.

"We were having this conversation is all I remember. I wanted to look at the sunset, I wanted to slow things down, I was expressing myself, there in the moment, I wanted us to talk about our feelings and—"

"Ugh," Robert groaned.

"Oh shit," said Wayne.

"And I was like, 'I want to deconstruct you.'"

"Deconstruct you!" Wayne howled.

"'I want to talk about your body, the way you smile, how you walk,' and I'm telling her this—"

"Jesus, Alan."

"For foke's sake," said Robert, lighting the bifter.

"Telling her she needs to get beyond herself, beyond her own needs, she needs to be more generous, more optimistic about human nature—"

"Goddamn Alan."

"Enough man."

"I'm telling her she has to feel and I can see in her eyes that she doesn't want to hear it, doesn't want to know it, she doesn't understand and doesn't even—"

"Alan, you got problems."

"Want to talk about the relationship—"

"Who the fuck does!" Wayne finally shouted, standing up and gathering his things.

Moments later we were back on our bicycles pedaling across meadows, around villages, past fields and through forests, following the slow brown bends and turns of the Warta. We reveled in the journey; we were there to exalt in it, to absorb it, drink it, bathe in it, which is why we harassed and interrupted each other as we dallied along the river like old ladies and slept in the grass like lapsed monks, talking and smoking and drinking and smoking more. You wouldn't call us men exactly, more like caricatures of men—curated versions of men, dressed up and stuffed the way pickled museum polyps on the wall are stuffed for future generations to inspect and sneeze at. Most of all we were caricatures of ourselves, doing everything possible to obliterate and mask ourselves in order to elongate the feeling of that gentle summer day—those soft velvety days when a man feels he has all the time in the world to become and to realize and achieve himself: to see a measure of progress amid those long perishable hours when death only eggs him on at a distance.

It was then, riding on the forest path headed east, that I asked myself in a voice resembling Abram's: *What is my progress, what is my form?* And as I sat up high on the grandfatherly Junker I imagined that I was, in fact, my grandfather again, yes, I had become my grandfather, I was him, Abram Mikhailovich, on my way home, bicycling east, trying to get back to the place where I had come from. As we passed old barns and decayed farmhouses, yards stacked high with logs and hay and orchards flush with trees bearing plums and cherries, I inhaled the smell of grass and cloddy soil that rose and fell in a sea around me. I could almost taste the meadows, the blond fields and dark pine groves under that azure sky as I remembered what it was to be a young man in Europe. And here, in the Polish backwater, along this dark river following a coarse trail to no-place villages named Sosnowiec and Barnoko, here was the experience of my grandfather that I'd come cycling back to reclaim, as if to gather him up in my arms then throw him—throw my entire past— into the air like ash and watch it all blow away.

In the late afternoon we reached a juncture. Facing a directional crisis, we got off the bikes to smoke a cigarette.

"The river's jost off there through the trees ain't it?" said Robert.

"But which way is it flowing? We got all turned around," said Wayne.

"Nobody's turned around," said Alan, looking up at the sky.

"It's flowin' *that* way and we need to go *that* way," said Robert.

"How is it you think we need to go *that* way?"

"Because that's where we're goin' if we're followin' the river."

"East, the river goes east, we need to go east. Rob, what's your compass say?"

Robert unbuttoned his shirt and revealed a scratched piece of plastic with an arrow dangling around his neck. He studied it. "That's east like ah said."

"Okay, let's just have us a bifter and think about—"

"No, let's get moving," said Alan who was already climbing back up on his rig. "The river was heading south but now it's heading east, is that it?"

"Yeh."

"So that's east?"

"That's north right up there, or what—"

"Where's the goddamn arrow pointing?"

"So we've been going the wrong way?"

"What do you boys think about a campsite right here?"

"Not a bad idea."

"Maybe over there's a little copse o' woods."

"Let's go check it out and maybe bed down for a smoke—"

"By the riverside—

"Right up here maybe—"

"Could just bale down—"

"In the morning we'll figure it out—"

"Let's just bike around and see—"

"How about right over there—"

"That ain't no clearing—"

"Or maybe just right up by the river there—"

"We could go a little bit further and get right along the banks—"

"This looks good, we're on the bend now—"

"This looks awesome—"

"If we just find a clearing—"

"That's what I was thinking, if we go a little bit along this way we can find—"

"All we want is a clearing."

We found our clearing. It was a perfect clearing. Level, beside the river, with a fire pit already built. We pitched tents and passed the grappa. Wayne got a bifter on the go as Robert stomped off through the woods to search for logs. We heard him crashing around the brush, it was getting dark, then we heard the axe hacking and a while later Robert returned like some primordial man covered in filth and sweat and dragging the giant limbs of trees behind him. We got a fire raging and by nightfall the flames were leaping above our heads, towering, soaring, burning high and hot into the night. We drank and smoked as the logs burned into a hundred shapes—"It's a pig's head," "It's a dog's head," "It's a shark," "It's a crucifix on fire!"—and our tuna pasta dinner became an afterthought as the flames absorbed us and the bone-colored moon rose up off the Polish plain into the marine night sky. We heard shouts and laughter coming from across the river where a party was under way; cars were wheeling up, men were chopping wood in the darkness, cutting and burning down a forest to feed their flames but their fire never grew as tall as ours because now we couldn't stop feeding what we'd started: We were locked to it, addicted to it, a primeval wind was blowing through our camp beside the swampy river edge, something lingering and hovering though we didn't know quite what. It was in the silky moon and sky and stillness, an almost tropical calm that smothered the air as our fire soared immense and we flung off our shirts then because it was so damn hot. We stood there jabbing the logs, hopping, dancing around the flames for one hour, two, all evening long we encircled and challenged and taunted the flames; we were wolves, we were warriors, drawn to the heat, inhaling the smoke, dodging the cracks in the silence and when we spoke it was only to discuss the fire, the aboriginal flame that we prodded with our thin branches, that we tormented, fought with, revered and determined to triumph over and eradicate: to eradicate the woods until there was nothing left in them to burn! The fire had enslaved us, it had mastered us there beneath the moon clinging white like a rose in the eastern sky as we erected ourselves against the primal element and refused to watch the embers burn out. Gripped by it, empty without it: The fire was all we had so we added more logs to the dying city whose embers flickered in an ocean of ash. The embers flashed and flared as they got absorbed in the hot gray dust and perhaps we recognized ourselves in the embers; we were sputtering and showering heat, too, the burning dying embers in a city of ash soon to be buried under more embers and more ash, yet so recent this fire, so bright and so brief and consumed without purpose. It was a funeral pyre burning in the woods—the pyre of our youth, of our intentions—and no matter what jokes and memories and buffooneries we told we could not escape the embers. So it was fitting then when Robert pulled from his sack a long thin wooden flute and began to play. He played it by the fire's orange light, in the shadow like some solemn sylvan rite or ritual that we didn't want to end, not the music or the fire or the moon or any of it. We wanted to dance and sit and laugh in that crackling silence, inhaling smoke and flames and ash and soot because it tasted good; because the singed bark and charcoal with the damp sweet river air tasted raw like silt and black sugar earth, it was a heavenly taste and like sharks we circled round the fire adding branches, building the flames higher, stoking the unquenchable thirst in us all to see it burn.

Sixteen

KGB Dues

Vilna, 2009

We parted in the tiny Polish town of Konin where the fellows hopped a train back to Berlin, taking my bike and gear with them as I rode the tracks east to Warsaw. When I arrived I had some hours to kill waiting for my connection, so I wandered the counterfeit streets of the old city. Warsaw stands on a hill, rather it's a kind of plateau that rises sharply off the Wisła River and leaves the city almost hanging there, framed between a roaring freeway and the sky. Warsaw is spooky: a network of movie-set alleys and false renaissance facades that are no substitute for the real thing. The real thing, of course, was obliterated in the war and since the Poles aren't all that interested in progress they attempted to hammer and plaster up a copy of the original. Museums honoring Poland's heroes clog the city center—houses dedicated to Frédéric Chopin and Adam Mickiewicz, Witold Gombrowicz and Marie Curie. But what they should have done is built one big museum for the City of Warsaw and put everything, the whole damn ruinous past, inside it. That way the Poles could have moved forward and created a new city—with a new self—instead of clinging to the hurt, trapped, stagnant spirit of morose nostalgia that remains the Polish identity today.

But I didn't come to pick apart the Poles. My family had little to do with the Poles. Poland was just the land between the places my family called home: Berlin to the west, Kovno to the east. The Poles played such a small role in my family's story, in fact, that I really should have nothing to say about them at all, but I do. With a vile days-old brew of grappa and vodka sloshing around my gut, I sat on a bench to watch the sun descend over glossy neo-ancient Warsaw and the truth is I was disappointed with the Ghetto. That famous place, cauterized like a cow brand on fifteen million Jewish minds, and what is it today? A few hectares of cement rubble clothed in earthen berms, virtually invisible, where nothing is preserved, nothing has been created and nothing remains, even, to imagine. The Poles went to the trouble to remake an entire faux medieval capital for chrissakes but they couldn't show a crumb of respect for the mother of all ghettos? Instead what I saw was callousness on the faces of the people walking past. The city made me nervous and it made me dry and anxious to leave it so after sundown I returned along the wide Soviet boulevards to the train station where I spent my last złotys on a bottle of warm Lech beer and settled into an open-air sleeper car that took me, via innumerable countryside stops, all the way to Vilna.

It was dawn when I reached the Lithuanian capital and since there wasn't much to do at that hour I stumbled through Vilna's old deserted streets past charming stone archways streaked in rose-colored morning light. I sat down and slept under one of them. It was a dazed sleep, one of those enchanting rests that overwhelms you, erases you almost, and when I awoke there were tourists with cameras hovering and the sun pierced my eyes. I hurried into a *kavarna* on Didžioji Street, asked for a coffee and washed my face in preparation for the appointment. Then, shortly after nine, I stepped into a cab and moments later found myself standing in the lobby of the Lithuanian State Historical Archives. I was greeted by Ms. Slovanowa, a jittery-voiced woman with a robust bosom and large behind who seemed personally offended that I had arrived without first submitting a lengthy questionnaire to determine whether or not they could help me. Ms. Slovanowa made long strides down the red-carpeted corridor as she led me to her office.

"I feel sympathy for people like you," she said, pointing me into the seat opposite her desk. "You travel thousands of miles from your home, you don't know what you're looking for and most of the time you find nothing, nothing at all." Her expression told me she had urgent jobs to do and mine wasn't one of them.

"I didn't know the questionnaire was necessary and wasn't sure which bureau—"

"I see." She reached for a blank piece of paper on her desk and picked up a pen. "Now tell me the names of your family, their birth dates, marriage dates, divorce dates, deportation dates, dates of death. Everything you know."

Ms. Slovanowa took notes based on my limited knowledge of Anton Isaakovich Grunefeld, his business and his deportation along with his children. She nodded with a distracted air, glancing up now and then with a tired, almost amused expression as if none of what I was telling her was new, it was the same story she had heard yesterday and the one she would hear tomorrow and isn't this an absurd and desperate situation we both know you're in: That is what her face was telling me. After a pause Ms. Slovanowa stood up. "Please go wait in the hall," she said and disappeared through a door behind her desk.

I returned to the hall and sank into the plastic burgundy creases of an armchair. Two elderly women were seated at tiny writing desks stationed along the corridor wall. One of the women was hunched over a document, making loud scratching sounds with a pencil, while the other was shuffling and reordering a stack of pages, and between the scratching and the shuffling and the corridor's dark stuffy archival air I sat bewildered, waiting for Ms. Slovanowa, wondering, What am I waiting for anyway, for a sliver of my past to be delivered to me? What difference can it possibly make, all these birth and death and deportation dates? I don't need numbers and facts—I need a human story, I need my family's experience!—and it occurred to me that perhaps Ms. Slovanowa was right: It was absurd and desperate for me to come here looking for it.

All of a sudden one of the doors in the corridor flew open and Ms. Slovanowa rushed out balancing a stack of clothbound binders in her arms. She hurried past me into her office and dropped the pile on her desk.

"Paulina, the mother of your grandmother," she said, gathering her breath as she examined a page from the first binder, "was born Pesha-Ita. She was the daughter of David-Shloma Benleizer-Orel Sambor, and his wife Bashe-Beile Bat Zelman, née Voshvidovski."

I looked dumbly at Ms. Slovanowa, struck by the wholly unfamiliar syllables.

"Pesha-Ita was born on October 5th, 1886, in Kovno, but for some reason the documents don't make clear—" Ms. Slovanowa paused, opening a second binder and scanning several pages of small typed text—"the Sambor family remained registered in a small town in the countryside north of Kovno, a town by the name of Dotnuva."

"Dotnuva?"

"It may be for tax reasons that they chose not to change residence. One cannot be sure. In any case the Sambors never registered in Kovno."

Dotnuva. I let the sound roll around my lips. Staccato but smooth, with a timbre of the provinces. *Dotnuva.* I watched as Ms. Slovanowa opened a third binder and began copying names and dates onto a scrap of paper. "These are the four of Pesha-Ita's thirteen siblings we have on record," she said. "Khaim-Leib, born 1888; Sara-Rokhel, born 1890; Gode

157

Knaia, born 1892; and Shmuel, born 1893."

She abruptly closed the third binder, opened the fourth and told me that my great-great-great-grandfather's name was Leizer-Orel Sambor. "That is it," she said, standing up to escort me out. "That is all I know."

"But about Anton and his daughter Josephine, can't you tell me anything?"

"Yes, yes, Mr. Krumm, surely there is more to learn about your family, but not here," she said, waving me away. "If you want to know more then you must visit the KGB Archive." Ms. Slovanowa hurriedly jotted down an address on the scrap of paper beneath my relatives' names. "Of course if you are so persistent you must go to Kovno," she added, glancing sharply over her glasses as she closed the door behind me.

* * *

The guard seated at the table next to the KGB elevator shaft was chewing on a toothpick, leafing through a tabloid. He seemed to be purposely ignoring me. I coughed and said, in German, "I'm here to see the chief archivist."

"The chief has gone to lunch. Come back later."

"Can I speak to his secretary?"

"Come back in an hour," he replied and his eyes returned to a photo of a car accident as the toothpick flicked angrily in his mouth. When I returned an hour later the guard was asleep, elbow on the table, chin in hand. He woke with a startle and handed me a tiny piece of paper, ripped from his tabloid, with a name written on it: "Neveris, KGB Archive." I walked out to Gedimino Prospect and began asking for directions. Most people glanced at the paper, gave a wary look and walked on. Finally an old man pointed me to the street, very close by, and when I approached the building I saw two men standing at the entrance enveloped in cigarette smoke.

"I'm looking for Mr. Neveris," I said.

The taller of the men eyed me severely, threw his half-smoked cigarette to the ground and turned to climb the steps. I followed. We made several turns through a long zig-zagging hallway, at the end of which we entered an office where the man said, in a deep voice with breath smelling of tobacco and fish, "I am Mr. Neveris."

Mr. Neveris had large dark circles under his eyes. He glanced frequently out the window onto the empty courtyard below as I repeated my family's story and the names in question. In the end he shrugged and said tiredly, "We no longer keep records here."

I didn't budge but instead asked for a fuller response. So Mr. Neveris, with a reluctant air, picked up the telephone, put it to his ear and dialed. His gravelly breaths rattled through the receiver between rings. Finally a voice answered and his macabre face lit into a half-smile. First the obligatory greeting. A joke. A forced laugh. Some personal exchange done in whispers. Then I heard my relatives' names spelled out, letter by letter. After some minutes Mr. Neveris shouted, "*Da! Da!* Okay," and hung up.

"You will go this afternoon to see the files," he said with a grave air. "Take bus 33 to the final stop."

* * *

The old bus coughed and growled, jolting with heaves of exhaust as it climbed out of central Vilna and made its way up a steep road of switchbacks past miles of gray apartment towers before it clattered to a halt at a field of tall weeds beside the freeway. I looked around. There wasn't a building or sign or any indication of where I should go. All I saw was a teenage boy walking in long strides through the waist-high grass. He was smoking a cigarette and staring with great con-

159

centration at the ground. When I stopped him to ask for directions he raised his head and squinted at the sun as though seeing it for the first time that day. With the gesture of a man twice his age, the boy took off his cap, raised his forearm to wipe his brow and turned about-face. The cigarette stayed glued to his lower lip as he led me several hundred yards, over a hill and out of the grassy thicket on to a road marked Oscar Milasiaus Avenue. The boy pointed at three gray buildings looming over the avenue like giant tombstones. "KGB," he said, spitting the butt on the ground and taking the five lita coin I held out to him.

Soldiers were standing guard outside the high-security glass doors when I approached. I didn't know which of the three buildings to enter; they were each replicas of one another. Suddenly I heard a shout in French. *"Monsieur!* You are the man of the Grunefeld family?" A young guard with a square face was walking quickly toward me.

He clasped my hand and said it was an honor to practice his French with a foreigner.

"I'm American."

"Je sais, je sais, but *Madame* does not speak a word of English or German or anything but Lithuanian," he said with a wink, "and Russian of course."

The guard led me to the central building. We proceeded through several dim passageways as he continued speaking in an animated *français* and regarding me with enthusiasm. *"Oui, oui, Monsieur Grunefeld,* everything has been prepared this hour. However it is getting late and our national holiday begins tonight, therefore you must see the documents quickly."

We entered a spacious archive room where the guard introduced me to a tiny woman with an unpronounceable name who I took to be *Madame.* She was seated behind an enormous desk with papers and parts of an egg sandwich scattered across it.

"The man is here to see about the Grunefeld family!" the guard announced, then turned and whispered to me with another wink. "*Je suis votre traducteur.*"

"Come, sit down," the woman said, studying my face with cloudy, suspicious eyes. She lifted her hand to her cheek and groaned. "*Madame* has bad tooth," said the guard. For a moment the woman and I sat there looking at each other, unsure who should speak first. Then she released her hand from her cheek, turned on her swivel chair and reached for two thin folders on the windowsill behind her. One of the folders was blue. The other was yellow. The woman saw my eyes anxiously following her movements and she reacted by moving even more slowly. She opened the blue folder and examined the first page, all Cyrillic, marked on the bottom with the red stamp of the KGB. Then *Madame* proceeded to read line by line from the page, a formal decree or official citation of some kind. The guard did his best negotiating the complicated text into French, then the woman turned to the second page, and by the third page I had had enough. I knew my minutes were dwindling.

"All of the pages, please," I told the guard. "I'd like to photocopy the full archive."

The woman rubbed her cheek and shook her head in that hopeless way the Soviets have of answering. She opened the yellow folder and turned to a page with a small black and white photograph affixed to it.

"It is the daughter of Anton Grunefeld?" she asked.

I took hold of the page and looked down at a pair of eyes blazing up into mine like two frightened embers. Aunt Josey's restless pupils pierced the photographic paper as if the whole miserable century was glaring out of them. I studied the flat boyish cheeks and the oval chin and the mouth that resisted expression. I saw my eyes in her eyes. I saw my expressionless mouth in her mouth. "*Da*," I nodded, "Josephine Antonovna Grunefeld."

The woman smiled gently as she patted her cheek. She looked suddenly more inspired and began turning the pages one after the next. Through the guard's translation she said, "This is an official notice... Here are the details of Mr. Grunefeld's business earnings... This page shows accusations made against Mr. Grunefeld... Here is the deportation decree. Which pages would you like to photocopy?"

"All of them!"

The woman shook her head again. "It is against state policy to copy the full archive. You may select individual material to photocopy, that is all."

"But how can I know which material I want to photocopy," I said, "when I can't even read it?"

"That is why I am reading to you what is written," she said.

I addressed the guard directly. "You said the office will close soon because of a holiday?"

"Yes," he replied with a beaming smile. "In forty five minutes it closes, then one week of holiday to celebrate crowning of King Mindaugas."

"So I need the photocopies now. There isn't time for her to read through every page telling me what each one says."

"How many photocopies do you want?"

"As many as you can make."

The guard leaned down close to *Madame*. They exchanged whispers. Finally he stood up. "Three euros per page," he said.

"Three euros!" I opened my wallet and saw I was just shy of sixty. I hadn't come prepared to be dragged through the mud by an archivist with a toothache extorting me for family documents. But there was no time to rush to a bank and I wasn't about to hang around Vilna for 10 days celebrating the

162

crowning of King Mindaugas. So I accepted defeat and bargained the *Madame* down to fifty eight euros for twenty two black-and-white photocopies. Fifty eight euros, I thought, to feed the keepers of the ex-KGB. Fifty eight euros to buy back my past.

"Now which pages?" said the guard.

"Oh oh oh!" moaned the woman, clutching her mouth. "You must hurry, what a terrible toothache!"

She opened the blue folder and as we rifled through the pages together, I chose them mostly on instinct. "This one here," I said, "that one too," and she drew a small red circle around the page numbers. The guard hunched over the desk assembling a pile of my chosen documents—requests, referrals, reports, memoranda, some pages handwritten, others typed. We hurried through the same process with the yellow folder, then the woman shuffled to the room's single photocopier and, while still patting her mouth, placed the twenty two pages inside the machine. As the copied pages came out she applied an official Lithuanian state seal to each. She handed me a release form to sign. Finally she put the pages in a large white envelope and pressed it to my chest as though it were a gift.

"I hope you find what you are looking for," she said.

I placed the fifty eight euros in her palm and for the first time saw the woman smile. A half dozen silver teeth glittered in her mouth.

"I hope your toothache feels better," I said, then waved *au revoir* to the guard and walked outside to wait for the bus that would carry me back down the mountain.

SEVENTEEN

THE MISSING CHILD

Kovno, 2009

I stared out the dirty window of the *marshutka* where I was squeezed in back alongside farmers and old women carrying baskets of vegetables on and off at muddy villages along the remote route to Kovno. The countryside was flat leaving Vilna and it remained that way, placeless somehow, as a steady rain soaked the brown fields. Two hours later the van lurched to a stop at the Kovno bus terminal, where I bought a city map from an old man sitting slouched against a kiosk, then started off walking toward Maironio Street. After twenty minutes in light rain I reached the street, which wasn't even a street but an alleyway. It led into a small parking lot and at the back of the lot stood a white building with a bronze plaque affixed to the wall indicating the Kovno Regional Archives.

I climbed a flight of stairs and entered a strangely barren office. Two computer monitors sat caked in dust on a narrow table along one wall. A few plants drooped in pots at the other end of the room. I thought I was alone until I approached a tall counter, peered over and saw a young woman in a red sweater with a telephone pressed to her shoulder. She had on glasses and her face was lit up by the pale green screen in front of her. The woman wasn't moving or saying a thing until the instant when her fingers exploded across the keyboard. "*Da!*" she said, hands typing furiously, "*Da! Da!*" and as she took down the dictation I noticed a grimacing pain on her face. I turned away and looked out the window at the steely sky looming over Kovno. Moments later the woman hung up the receiver and I peered back over the desk as her dark eyes rose to meet mine. She had soft, intelligent features, somewhat homely and attractive at the same time, with sand-colored hair that fell past her shoulders. Her long eyelashes and two sizeable dimples in her cheeks signaled welcome. "Thank you for your patience," she said in confident English. "It has been busier today than normal. How may I help you?"

"Do you get many people here asking about their family history?"

"Sometimes, though not much recently. Mostly it is bureaucratic work. But my passion is history. Is that why you are here, to learn about your past?"

"Yes."

"You are the first this week," she said, studying me with curiosity. "You are American?"

"Yes. Tell me, isn't this a holiday?"

"Oh yes, many people in my country celebrate the anniversary of the crowning of King Mindaugas, but many people also work. I must work," she said. The grimace like a shot of pain returned to her face. "Rather, I prefer to work."

"You prefer work?"

"My work allows me to help people. I like to assist those who are here to learn about their past. If I can help one person know his past it makes me feel, how can I say... useful. I was recently helping a Russian—"

"The Russians come here? I thought they're not welcome."

"Yes, often they call but sometimes they come, too, and you are right, it is strange because many Russians are now coming and officially we hate the Russians, but I have different feelings because I have learned so much from their culture, I have read their literature and admired their art and music, there is so much richness—"

"Your English is incredible. You must have gone abroad to study."

"No, I learned it here in school and in my job. I traveled once to England but it was only for two weeks and that was many years ago. Tell me please, what is your name?"

The woman's eyes were wide and searching. They invited warmth but there was something hurting in them as well. She winced once more, this time pressing her hand against her left hip.

"Max Krumm. But tell me, are you alright? You seem in pain."

"Oh, it is nothing," she said, shifting in her seat, "only the rheumatism. It aches sometimes. My family, we have all gotten it quite young, I am thirty four but…. oh, oh," she said, clenching above her thigh. "It isn't a problem, I will go to the doctor after lunch and receive an injection. It makes me feel better and allows me to work." Her smile returned with renewed focus. "My name is Vitalya. Now tell me, Max, how may I help you to know your past?"

I reached into my pack, pulled out my journal and unwrapped the two layers of plastic covering the postcard. I handed it to Vitalya. After she had read it I told her everything I knew: names, cities, dates of birth and deportation. Vitalya stood up and with some effort pulled a heavy folder off the shelf. It contained a jumble of architectural maps showing all the properties that had ever been owned in Kovno, listed in alphabetical order by owner. She flipped through the pages, arrived at the letter G, and within moments found what she was looking for. She wrote out the house's address and handed it to me.

"Here is a start, Max. This way you can visit the former home of the Grunefelds while I go to see the doctor. I will return in the afternoon and we can speak further, yes? I hope by then to have other information for you."

"Thank you, Vitalya."

"Please, call me Vitya."

* * *

I got lost for an hour wandering through the old city until I arrived at the squat cement structure at Duonelaicio Street #9. The walls were dull stucco gray, marred by swaths of mold and graffiti. Cracks in the plaster ran from the street all the way up to the roof. On the second floor was a large circular window with two smaller, oval-shaped ones beneath it. The decidedly modernist structure was built, according to documents, by one Georgis Ilynienes in 1934. The following year, the lease was signed by the building's first renter, a widower Jew who with his children had recently relocated from Berlin and owned an electrical goods store on Kovno's principle boulevard, Laisves Aleja.

I stood across the street gazing at the building, studying its decay as I tried to imagine the warm June night when Josephine gripped Evgeny's hand and followed her father out the door, down the steps and into the trucks that were waiting to take them to police headquarters. Finally I crossed the street and pressed the buzzer. Silence. Then a pattering of steps, feet rushing downstairs. The door opened and two men dressed in matching khaki shirts and ironed slacks stood eyeballing me.

"Good afternoon," I said, trying both German and English. "My family used to live here."

After an awkward handshake the men welcomed me inside. We stood in the coat room and I noticed both men shifting nervously on their feet as I attempted to communicate the reason for my visit. They had trim moustaches and they stood with matching postures: hands on hips, squinting slightly with expressions that seemed to take in little of what

I was saying. I pointed at my eye with a universal gesture, and said, "May I look around?" The men stared at me in dismay. After a few whispers, they fled together up the staircase and left me standing alone in the foyer with no choice but to explore the house on my own.

It looked no different from the typical German homes of the era: tall ceilings, hardwood floors, spacious rooms with lots of light. Some of the rooms had been converted into modern offices and there was a crisp, clean feel to the place. But the past, for me, overwhelmed the present as I saw Anton returning home in the evening, hanging his jacket by the front door and entering through the living room. Evgeny, sitting at the piano with his back to the side wall, let his fingers glide gently across the keys while Josephine reclined with a book on the sofa seat beneath the window. Fine art covered the walls, perhaps the smell of borscht was wafting from the kitchen and in the dark-stained cabinet behind its delicately carved doors sat the family saucers and silverware and—

"I am engineer," a man's voice spoke loudly behind me. I turned to see the two fellows who were now joined by a third, smaller, bristly-faced man in a striped turquoise shirt and jean vest. The obvious master of this troika, he extended his hand with formality. "What reason for your visit?" he squeezed out the words in English. The three men surrounded me in a triangle as though ready for a rugby scrum.

"This house once belonged to my family," I said.

The man studied my eyes. He gave a thoughtful, timid smile as he exchanged glances with his colleagues. Then he leaned forward and, in a hushed voice, said: "You have......interest......to take......building?"

Six anxious, colorless eyes fixed on mine as the men stood with bated breath. I looked at the engineer, baffled by his question, and when he couldn't hold his tongue any longer he tried again.

"You want......to have......building......of......family?"

At that moment I realized what I'd failed to see, and laughed. "No, no, comrades! I don't want the building," I said, waving my arms to clear away the fog of miscommunication. "I'm not here to reclaim any building for my family. I only want to look at it—to *see* it, that is all."

The men disbanded their triangle and retreated into an even tighter huddle, whispering and consulting with dead serious expressions. At last I heard a laugh. It came from the chief engineer and upon seeing him relax his companions looked at one other, then at me, before letting out a healthy whoop. All three of the men were now laughing and I was laughing with them, affirming our new camaraderie. The chief then undid the top button of his vest and invited me to his office. I could still hear some hiccupping laughter as I followed the men up a staircase that opened on to a large, empty room with a high yellow ceiling. There was a short corridor—what must have been the hallway, with Josephine's and Evgeny's rooms on either side—and at the end of that stood an office. I peeked in and saw a group of gray-haired men with dark suits and heavy eyes sitting around a table. A Moorish-style archway had been carved into the plaster doorway, adding an exotic element to the house. The floor's other side featured a balcony with a spectacular view over Kovno. The engineer led me out to the balcony and left me alone for a few minutes as I tried to picture the view through their eyes. I wanted the place to belong to Anton and Josephine and Evgeny again. I wanted them to inhabit it and to replay for me the everyday details of their lives—what familial sounds had stirred there, what smells and tastes, what temperatures, voices and shades of light had given life to the Grunefeld home before that fateful night when it ended and they were sent east. I gazed as though onto another century as I stared out across the worn rooftops and spires of Lithuania's former capital. When the chief engineer returned, he stood by my side with a nervous look and began to fidget so I thanked him for his time and nodded to the two gentlemen in khaki, then descended the staircase and walked back out on to Kovno's gray streets in search of the delightful rheumatic archivist.

When I returned to the archives, however, Vitya was nowhere to be seen. Instead there was a handwritten note, taped to the locked office door, which read:

> Max,
> I found something in the Grunefeld file that I do not understand, but you might! I want to tell you as soon as possible. I will not return to work after my visit to the doctor, instead let us meet at 8 o'clock this evening at Café Metropolis on Laisves Aleja. I will explain to you then.
> Vitya

My dear investigator Vitya! What fortune had allied us with your luminous eyes, your button-sized dimples and your crippled gait? I pulled the note off the door and stuck it in my journal a few pages from Aunt Josey's postcard. The rain had stopped, there was still enough light for a walk, so I strolled out to the edge of Kovno where the Neris and Nemunas rivers met at a marshy, angular embankment. I waited while the sky grew darker, then I returned to the city center, found Café Metropolis where my great uncle had played during his young brilliant years, and stepped inside the club.

I spotted her instantly. She was sitting under a low-hanging lamp in the corner of the cafe. Papers were sprawled across the dark oak table. A half-drunk cup of coffee revealed the ruby markings from her lipstick. I raised my hand at first, but seeing her outstretched fingers I instinctively took hold of them and leaned down to kiss her cheek in greeting.

"Did you find the home?"

"Yes," I said, giving her a summary of the engineers. "Are you feeling better?"

"Oh yes, in fact I probably didn't even need to go for the injection although it always feels better after." Then her eyes flashed hot. "Max, I found information for you."

"You have already done a lot for me."

"No, it is not much, if you only knew about my family, if I told you the stories of my grandfather and grandmother— oh, I must write it down one day but if I told you—"

"Your family, were they—"

"Not now, Max," she interrupted, "this is not time to talk about my family because we are here to talk about yours. Now you see I started by looking at the interrogation transcripts from your great grandfather Anton Grunefeld." Vitya pushed three hand-written pages across the table. "Here are the records of Grunefeld's final conversations with the authorities before he was deported. And here are the typed accusations against him regarding his store on Laisves Aleja."

I glanced up at the waiters who were rushing around delivering coffee and cakes to the mostly young clientele. A black piano sat unplayed on a raised wooden platform near the café entrance. Was it so different, I wondered, seventy years ago?

"But here is what I found that I think will interest you most, Max, although I am not sure I understand it. You talked about a family connection in the village of Dotnuva."

"Yes."

"But it was many years before the war that your family moved from Dotnuva to Kovno?"

"Yes."

"You said your grandmother's sister, Josephine Grunefeld, returned here from Prague in 1938?"

"Yes."

"The records show that she was deported with her father and brother on June 16, 1941."

"Yes."

"That is not all."

"No?"

"There is a baby."

"A baby?"

"Yes, there is a baby," Vitya repeated.

"What do you mean? What baby? Whose baby?"

"There is a baby named Alexander."

"*Whose baby?*"

"I expect it is Josephine's baby."

"Josephine never had a baby."

"There is a baby registered in 1939 in Dotnuva under the name Alexander Abramovich Grunefeld."

"Alexander Abramovich!"

"Yes."

"Alexander Abramovich?"

"Yes! Who was Abram?"

"My grandfather. Are you sure Josephine was the mother of this Alexander Grunefeld? Surely there were other Grunefelds."

"We cannot be sure. Josephine was not the only Grunefeld woman living in Kovno at the time. But Max, this is what I do not understand: The baby is registered in Dotnuva, yet there is no birth certificate. Nothing. All registrations were accompanied by birth certificates. This means that the person who registered the baby may not have been his mother."

I stared out the café window at the dark street while repeating those eight syllables that made sudden inexplicable sense: *Alexander Abramovich.*

"There is more. You said the deceased mother of your grandmother was named Sambor?"

"Yes."

"I checked and there was one Sambor living in Dotnuva in 1939."

"Yes?"

"Sara-Rokhel Sambor. Perhaps she was an aunt, or a cousin. Maybe she took care of the baby while Josephine lived in Kovno. There is no way to know. But the record shows that Sara-Rokhel was killed by the Nazis at the Ninth Fort on August 3, 1941."

"What happened to the baby?"

"We cannot know."

"Why not?"

"There is no record."

"No record that he was killed or no record that he survived?"

"Nothing beyond his registration."

"So it is possible that he survived."

"It is possible, but the Nazis killed so many, hardly any Jews survived, and as a baby—"

"Vitya," I said, leaning in close, "I am going to Dotnuva."

"Yes."

"It's in the farm country not far from here?"

"Yes."

"Will you take me there?"

"Yes," she said, "Yes, I will."

Eighteen

Sleeping With the Dead

The road out of Kovno followed the Nevėžis River north across a flat green expanse of wheat and potatoes. Vitya had fallen asleep and her head bounced against my shoulder each time the bus shuttered to a halt: first in the small town of Babtai, then in the city Kedainiai, and finally when it pulled into the 700-person village of Dotnuva. On a lawn in the center of town stood a hulking red church, all brick and mortar, with baroque towers thrusting two oxidized lime-green onion domes into the sky. Vitya was walking slowly, limping at first as she steadied her left hip with her hand. She tried to conceal the pain but her grimace walked ahead of her. A warm afternoon wind was blowing across the fields, petting down the wheat like a painter licking them with his brush. As we passed some of the town's old unpainted wooden homes—white lace curtains hanging in the windows, sleepy gardens filled with tomato and bean plants, short neat stacks of firewood piled in the yards—I felt the past like a wave surge around me. It was everywhere: in the gold-toothed women wearing head scarves and flower-print dresses who chatted by the roadside selling pickles and mushrooms and buckets of cherries; in the deep bellowing of the cows from nearby meadows, and in the shouts of children dancing and fishing around a small dock beside a stream. The past was everywhere or perhaps my mind was simply overripe to imagine it, famished as I was for a sign, any sign or unseen hand to reach out and drag me back, as the Kaiser said, into the drowned chapters of history. I wanted back to my ancestors' world; back to the world I had been thinking about, and had been ruled over, for as long as I could remember. I wanted back to Alexander's world, to Alexander himself—but no! So many were murdered at the Ninth Fort and once the killing started in the summer of 1941 it didn't stop. It went on day and night, week after week. They would shoot uninterrupted for a half hour, an hour, two hours, half a day, then take a break for some cigarettes and *schnaps* before they went on shooting more. The sounds of rifle and machine gun shooting never stopped, they never let up from morning to night and when the Nazi soldiers couldn't stand the killing any longer, when they couldn't stand the smell of burnt flesh and bodies rotting in the trench, then they sent in boys to spread lime across the crumpled corpses before they went and shot some more. Yes, so many murdered, nearly all of them murdered, but a few survived and might that little boy have been one of them? Is it preposterous to think such thoughts? I wondered as I looked into the distant fields. Might someone in this village or in another village nearby have saved the boy, and might that boy have grown up into a man, and aged into a father, a grandfather even, and might he be looking out the window of one of these small white-curtained homes right now, looking out at the man who is standing on the road, on the other side of his destiny?

What had they done anyway in this little village, the Sambors and others of their kin? I wondered as I stared across the patchwork of unremarkable potato fields. Were they traders? Did they embroider? Were they craftsmen working in metals, or as printers, as tailors, bakers, teachers, butchers? Did they distill liquor? Did they trade in grain, timber, cattle or fish? In musk or aloe, camphor, cinnamon and honey? Maybe they collected tolls or managed a rich man's estate. Perhaps they were peddlers, smugglers of foodstuffs and goods for war. They might have been showmen traveling with the fairs; they might have posed as quacks and soothsayers, or possibly they played music with the *klezmorim*. Whatever the Sambors and their kind had for skills then surely those skills were portable: portable skills to generate portable wealth, yes, they lived portable lives and they preserved a portable religion which they carried with them along with the castor oil and linens and animal skins strapped to their backs. Although they didn't carry it all and trade it *fast enough*. Alexander! Where are you? Your mother left you here in order that you should live. She thought she would perish. Instead she survived, and I am the one now searching for your remains.

I turned, aware suddenly that Vitya was no longer behind me. She was standing in the distance on the lawn beside the church gazing up at the baroque towers. I walked toward her and asked her to accompany me to the small white monastery that stood behind the church, where I knocked on the door. It opened. A fat priest with a long black beard stood looking at me. He was wearing a striped gown and a skullcap and in his arms was a handsome black cat that he was massaging behind the ears. The priest didn't invite us in and he seemed impatient to know our business. I asked, with Vitya translating, whether he knew much history about the place. He shook his head.

"What I know is that the Russians burned this monastery down in the middle of the 19th century," he said.

"Do you know something about the Jews who lived in Dotnuva before the war?"

"That I cannot say."

"Did you ever hear of any survivors here?"

"I'll tell you, the Jews were never welcome in Lithuania although they have been here for as long as we can remember. The Jews are a tragic people. They wear the mark of Judas on their heads."

I could sense the priest studying my head for the mark of Judas so I asked him one last time: "Then you know nothing about any of the Jews from Dotnuva, whether any stayed, whether any of their children survived, where they might have gone?"

"They took them all away! They took them to the Ninth Fort, where do you think they took them? Not all of them, of course. No one can say for certain that they got all of them. Some were hidden. Some fled and survived in the forests. Sometimes the children were taken in and raised by families."

"Can you tell me which families, which ones took them in, because I'm looking—"

"I know nothing!" the priest cut me off. "And the people of Dotnuva know nothing and will tell you nothing either. Do not speak about the past, young man, do not ask them to remember what is over and what happened such a long time ago." With that the priest lowered the cat to the ground, raised his eyebrows as though he had suddenly remembered an important thing he had to do, and closed the heavy door.

* * *

It was evening and our bus was returning along a narrow country road from Dotnuva when, six miles north of Kovno, we crossed a freeway and Vitalya told the driver to stop; we got out, the trucks were roaring and the sky was darkening as we crossed over a wide earthen berm and entered the field which didn't feel much like a fort at first, it felt like any other field, except as we got closer I saw there was a giant trench dug deep down in it and the trench was encircled by an even deeper moat, a big hexagonal moat that you could look straight down into from the rim wall of the field and there was a plaque etched on the rim wall that said, "Near this wall Nazis shot and burned people in 1943-4," and it was easy enough to see gazing down at the moat how the bodies had been shot and buried there because you could still make out the black burn marks in the earth, marks that were still visible even in the dim light and I thought I smelled a gray ashen stench that was hanging in the air too, "Probably the smell will hang there forever," I said, but Vitalya was hanging on to me and she wasn't smelling anything, the grimace was off her face and in the faint light of dusk we trod over the fort's remains as she asked, "Do you want to go inside?" and I nodded so we walked around the wall perimeter onto an earthen mound that rose up into the fort and that is where I helped Vitya climb the iron gate, after which I climbed it too and once we were standing in the fort between the trenches I thought: How bizarre all these days and years that I've been traumatized by the past, perhaps unhinged, likely in shock, certainly fearful, and I told Vitya this and I told her that I wanted to leave, I wanted to get out then and there and catch a ride to Klaipeda where I could flee by boat from this place but she told me in a soothing voice, "No, Max, it is too late now," and I asked, "Too late for what?" and she said, "Too late for leaving, it is too late for everything," and I answered, "But Vitya, I'm feeling—" and she stopped me with her soothing voice that said, "Just stay here with me, Max, stay awhile because you need to feel this place now that you are here, now that you have come you need to see it, breathe it," and she was stroking my arm as she told me this but I said, "Vitya, I can barely see a thing any more," and she said, "You must think about it and remember it, Max, remember it for those—" "For those what!" I said, "For whom should I remember it, for Josephine's baby, for Alexander should I remember? I'll never know about Alexander and all the Alexanders and what might have been," and Vitya said, "No, you'll never know but just think about it and remember it, for all of us," and her voice felt smooth like soap rubbed across my sweated body as I looked at her, staring into Vitya's dark eyes which had become darker with the night and which were smiling with the night, sad and clear and like a rainy season they were smiling and that is when I inhaled her breath and bent my head to reach her mouth as her warm body sank into mine and her weight pressed into mine, she gave hers to mine, those rheumatized hips she was relinquishing as the last of light was vanishing, everything was vanishing and I laid Vitya on the grass and soil still warm from the sun, soil where the ancestors had lain with their blood spilling dry and cold then in a moment I made a thrust and vigor and was reclaimed between her legs, so mad and tiresome that lonesome thrust and vigor for I couldn't see her face but I imagined Vitya's dark eyes closed and I heard her breath as it rose and mixed with the sighing of the trucks that went tearing past while we went swimming through the flesh joining bone deep into the swimming return—Return to Omphalos where we were dripping and I was entering and all was drinking in the Return when suddenly she felt a chill, I felt a chill, a shivering warm great chill and breathed a deep fresh breath of night air unlike another, it was an exorcising air that tore me and replaced me as I was thrusting through the chill and through Vitalya, through the raw primeval of the hunted past until, in the darkness, I warmed and it was the gushing of the seed inside her, the seed that planted history the seed and many seeds which I delivered then to earth blood earth it was slopping all around me in the moonlight it was slopping with the serum shine on blood soaked earth and it was perverse, oh lord it was perverse that was disposable but Vitalya she was silent, perhaps she was enraged or perhaps relieved that the soil was ours together now, this tortured ash and silence it was ours so I put my arm around her and with drifting eyes I wondered, Is it a crime to sleep with the dead, with the ghosts of thousands upon tens of thousands who will disturb us, who will pester us the way my dead ancestors pestered, but then don't I have a right, I thought, to sleep in the deathbed of my past even if these ancestors are not my own, even if Alexander's blood is here or if it isn't, and I was determined sleep would not haunt me so I lay peaceful there with Vitya in my arms, close and peaceful in the warm night that covered like a blanket over the graves of the decomposed, there were bones and bullets and skulls on the rolling Baltic farmland and Yes, I thought, I have walked in the fields of my fathers and I shall sleep in the bedroom of the dead, so we surrendered thoughts and closed our eyes to the stars and dreamt, sounds never waking our deep and mournful sleep until light and birds of morning and the fresh cold air woke us in the breeze, we were wet, we were glitter, there was dew and earth and we were glowing like the fields lit red at dawn as we rose and climbed up back onto the embankment, scrambling out of the bedroom as the Ninth Fort wobbled like a conquered fire beneath us and Vitalya beside me walking strong and able, there was nothing I could say to her or ever wanted more for I had my balls back, "I will return," I said, "I cannot stay, I must go," and she said, "Yes, I know," then in moments we were on the road where cars trickled past the shadow of the fort and Vitya held her arm high as a van slowed, door ajar, then the woman turned and pressed one last stained kiss into my mouth with the whites of her dark eyes slipping backward until the van door closed and I, standing with my bag, shivering on the road, breathing interrupted, leapt the lanes and raised my thumb as five cars passed before there came a truck, it was a small truck, my favorite kind of truck—it was an ice cream truck—leaving Kovno for the sea and the man inside it said, "Klaipeda we go, you catch big ship!" and I smiled as the man shouted and the engine strained and the sun traced its morning arc across the sky, there were forests waving and farms rocking like a gentle sea and roads peeling back into townships plain as all the places our ancestors once built and it made me chuckle, the man's like for football, he was short and bald with muscles driving and he grasped the air with choppy sounds to find the words, his ploughman's fingers yearning form because it's what he had to do and what I had to do, to conjure form, for my hunger it had returned the way a wave hits sand, with ferocious clarity and memories awakened by a story someone is about to tell.

Acknowledgments:

Thank you to Berliners Keith Becker, Ralf Boent, Yaotzin Botello, Jacek Duchownik, Michael Dumiak, David Gawthorpe, Dave Graham, Carlos Jesús González, Itai Lahat, Micha Koch, Philipp Lichterbeck, Eric Marx, Kevin McAleer, Wolfgang Pomrehn, Karl Sandoval, Jacek Slaski and Peter Zilahy. I hope you may find a bit of yourselves in these pages.

Thank you to Alexa Dvorson, Nathaniel Eaton, Carmen Eller, Julian Kissman, Elad Lapidot, Sam Loewenberg, Audrey Mei, Riki Rebel, Gellert Tamas and Florian Werner, for reading various versions of this manuscript.

Thank you to Tod Thilleman and the team at Spuyten Duyvil, for getting this past the finish line.

Thank you to Benoit Brisbois, Buddy Bolton, Shelly Browning, Marilyn Cannon, Alessandro Cosmelli, Brian Dowd-Uribe, Sara Green, Noah Haglund, Julien Harrison, Nancy Hayssen, Stephen Kessler, Robert Leslie, Dustin Luther, Jim Mascolo, Nick Levitin, Marina Levitina, Natasha Levitina, Christine Levitin-Breyette, Katherine Meyering, Ken Nash, Ian Olds, Irene Pascual, Josep-Maria and Marisa Pascual Molinas, Daniel Polley, Pamela Porter, Rachel Rabkin Peachman, Matti Rautkivi, Heather Rawson, Jacob Resneck, John Schak, Joel Serino, Santiago Solari, Michael Stoll, Lauren Taubman, Barbara Thomson, Ethan Vlah, Jonathan Wettstein and Beagan Wilcox, for your enduring friendship and support.

Thank you to Karina Ioffee, for your passion and patience.

And thank you most of all to my mother Barbara Baer, father Alexis Levitin and stepfather Michael Morey, for your strength of character, your encouragement and love, and for inspiring me to pursue the life I wanted.

MICHAEL LEVITIN was born in Maine in 1976 and grew up in northern California. He studied history at the University of California, Santa Cruz, and earned his Masters degree from the Columbia Graduate School of Journalism. His writing has appeared in *The Atlantic*, *The Guardian*, *Los Angeles Times*, *Newsweek* and *Time*, among other publications. He was co-founding editor of the *Occupied Wall Street Journal* and founding editor of the *Prague Literary Review*. He lives in Berkeley, California, with his partner and daughter. This is his first novel.

Made in the USA
Middletown, DE
30 January 2019